THE FAE QUEEN'S CAPTIVE

A PECULIAR TASTES NOVEL

SIERRA SIMONE

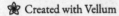 Created with Vellum

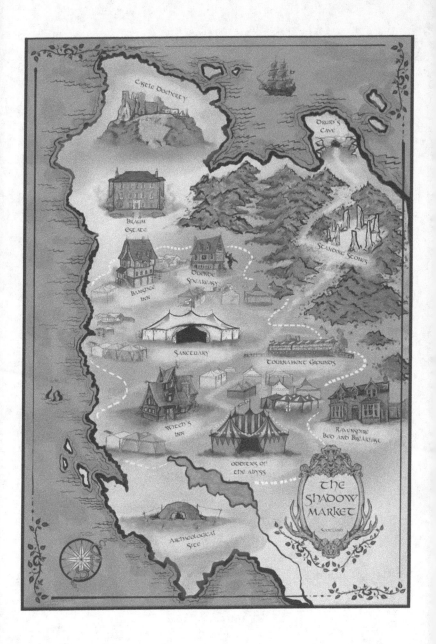

CONTENT WARNINGS

Violence, murder (of baddies), captivity, blood, explicit sex, hunting, intoxication, and uneven power dynamics.

CHAPTER 1

There are lights around the grave.

I press my face closer to the old farmhouse window and squint through its waves and ripples, willing the lights to resolve into something that makes sense. The lights flicker and jump like fire would, but it must be the distance playing tricks, because they *can't* be fire. It's an archaeological site, for one thing, all damp earth and plastic totes waiting to be filled with the last of the season's finds tomorrow, and for another thing, I was just there twenty minutes ago. It was utterly deserted then, empty of students and site managers and everything but the wind and the gaping mouth of the chambered cairn.

So. There should not be lights around the grave.

"What the bally hell are you doing?" says a voice from behind me. I turn to see one of my fellow grad students, Alfie, winding a thin caramel-colored scarf around his neck. It looks like it was sold by a company with a royal scarf warrant.

"There are lights by the cairn," I say, turning back to the window. The lights hover off the ground, surrounding the massive turf-covered mound of the grave and only leaving a gap where its entrance beckons.

"It's probably the fair, darling," Alfie says blithely. "Casting reflections or something."

"It's not the fair," I say without looking at him or in the direction of the carnival that appeared on the other side of the hill today.

Two of the other students went to investigate during our lunch break and found the place utterly devoid of people. Only the tattered booths and time-faded tents were there, lights already blinking and music already playing from somewhere unseen. The carousel of horses, peacocks, and rabbits turning in slow, riderless circles.

It looked abandoned and very murdery, one of the students said when they got back. And then they'd promptly enlisted as many of us as they could to return tonight.

"They could be fairy lights," Alfie says after a minute, looking out the window with me.

"Fairy lights?"

"My grandmother is Scottish," Alfie explains. "Always sticking silver in a baby's hand or planting rowan trees in her garden. And she says sometimes you can still see fairy lights at night. If you're in the right place, of course. Teine-sith."

Teine-sith.

The words sound familiar—or more so the sound of them. *Tyen-uh shee.*

Teine for fire. Sith for fairies.

"Gaelic, you know," Alfie says, with a toss of his floppy hair and the air of someone confiding a great secret. Then he seems to notice my lack of coat. "Are you not coming with us?"

I shift on my feet, torn. I love fairs—and people—and Halloween especially. But tomorrow is the very last day of the dig, and if someone is trampling all over our things, poking where they shouldn't, it could screw with our chances of keeping our permit for the next digging season.

And we have to come back next season because we still haven't found what we're looking for in this narrow, loch-floored valley.

"I think I should go check on the site," I say finally. And then I sigh a little, looking at the far hill with its ridges outlined by the carnival lights glowing behind it. I can already taste the popcorn, hear the pling of the high-striker bell. There's even supposed to be a haunted house...

"Look, it's probably some youths making Halloween mischief at the tomb, like their grandparents before them, and *their* grandparents before them," Alfie says, taking my hand and saying *youths* like we aren't twenty-three ourselves. "Don't be a bore. Who else is going to convince François that I'm his soul mate and he needs to whisk me away to Provence for a sun-soaked movie montage? This is my time of need!"

"It pains me," I say as I hold his gloved hand with both of my own, "since I've been needing you two to move past the Longing Glances Across the Dig Site phase for months now. But if it *is* locals down at the cairn, then you know I really do have to go check it out."

"Can't we call Dr. Siska and have her come instead?" Alfie whines.

"She and the site managers are staying twenty minutes away, and that's by car. I'm a short walk away. I'll just nip down there, shoo everyone off the site, and then I'll come to the fair after that and find you all. Deal?"

Alfie pouts. "Fine. But if I'm denied my great French love affair because you care more about some long-dead Spaniard's missing castle than you do your very best friend, I shall never forgive you."

I kiss his suntanned forehead through his wavy hair. "I'll only be a moment. Tell everyone to go on without me."

"As you wish. And don't eat the fairy fruit," Alfie says, cheerful again as he pulls away.

"*What?*"

"You know, if you're taken by the fairies," he explains patiently, straightening his gloves. "You're not supposed to eat the fairy fruit. It drives us mortals wild with desire. Or did you not read any Victorian poetry at school?"

"I know about fairy fruit!" I say, wounded. I'm practically a fairy pomologist. Or at least I should be, after all the fan fiction I read as a teenager. "But I don't think it's going to be a problem tonight. Or any night, given that fairies aren't real."

"How someone digging for a long-lost castle can be such a cynic is beyond me." Alfie sighs, and with a final pitying look, he goes downstairs to join the carnival sortie.

Sometimes it's beyond me too, Alfie.

With my own sigh, I find my jacket and a scarf, grab my phone and my headlamp, and shove on my muddy dig boots. Just before I leave, however, I stop by the bound photocopy sitting on my end table.

Hugo de Segovia was a captain of the 1588 Spanish Armada—or at least he was until he was shipwrecked on the shore just a mile away. His record of his time in the armada was rediscovered moldering in some archives just a few years ago, and from there, it had found its way to Dr. Siska, a specialist in Iron Age and medieval fortifications. She's been using de Segovia writing to search for a missing castle ever since. Thus why we're all here sifting through the cold Scottish mud, finding neolithic settlements instead of castle foundations, despite the initially promising ground surveys.

I pause—Alfie's words echoing in my mind—and I pick up the photocopy before flipping quickly through the densely typewritten pages, scanning between the original Spanish and the English translation.

Teine-sith.

I knew the word sith the minute Alfie had spoken it. Sith —or sidhe—is the Gaelic word for fairy, and fan fiction aside, my undergraduate thesis was centered on the archaeological remnants of ritual and superstition in medieval Scotland...and medieval written references to fairies were often rendered in Gaelic—when they weren't rendered as daemones in Latin or as elves in English.

But it wasn't until Alfie spoke the word aloud that something clicked for me. Hugo de Segovia hadn't spoken Scottish Gaelic—not a word of it—and so he'd spelled out the words as he'd heard them.

Tyenha xii.

THE LORD, in his good pleasure, had not delivered our ship from the storm, even as we saw the others blown over the horizon. But we were cast upon the shore of a wild place, and there we cried to the Virgin for help, but no help came.

A priest did come upon us, and in Latin he said he could do nothing for us, because it was the equinox and the lights would be on the hill, and it was safe for no man, woman, or child to see the lights. When we asked what manner of lights should be dangerous, he could only name them in his own tongue, tyenha xii, and then exhorted us to go south along the beach until we reached the next village, where we could perhaps smuggle ourselves back to Flanders or home to Spain. But the mist came, and with it the dark, and when we came upon lights at last, they belonged not to a village but to a castle of such luxury, presided over by a great lord, who welcomed us with food and wine and also spoke in Latin to us, and spoke a great many other languages besides, including our own tongue...

. . .

DR. SISKA LED this dig hoping to find evidence of Hugo de Segovia's lost castle, and so we focused on the geographically relevant details of his writing—the heading of his ship during the storm and descriptions of the beach and the castle. It's known from his account that he finally made it to Oban— alone—dazed and telling stories of his men imprisoned inside a castle made of silver and mist, and so from Oban and the beach, Dr. Siska had triangulated the identifying details to this lonesome spot in the Highlands, a valley near the coast, freckled with neolithic tombs and standing stones.

But she had not—nor had any of us—paid much mind to the priest's warning about lights on the hill. That a sixteenth-century Scottish priest would be superstitious is hardly surprising, and anyway, it seemed evident the lights must have belonged to the castle and not any supernatural powers tied to the equinox.

But now, as I'm looking at the lights flickering around the grave outside, the dead priest's words seem *very* relevant. Perhaps Alfie was right and the lights tonight are from some local tradition—even if that tradition is half-drunk young people daring themselves to get close to the local haunted hill. A folk memory preserved as fun and games. Perhaps it was a folk memory even in de Segovia's time.

Either way, I can't have people tramping around our dig site, no matter what Halloween customs they have around here. Several of the totes are filled with unfired sherds begging for a chance to crumble back into clay; half the grids still need photographed so we know where we've been when we come back next year. And above all else, we have to leave Historic Environment Scotland a pristine, well-conserved site, without even a rogue stake or Maltesers wrapper, so they won't revoke our permission to dig next year.

I toss de Segovia's account onto my bed, zip up my coat, and step out into the velvet-dark night to walk to the ancient grave. It'll be quick work, and then I'll be at the fair having fun: exactly the kind of Halloween night I deserve.

CHAPTER 2

The farmhouse where the grad students have been bunking is set higher in the valley, and the eternal Scottish wind fusses at my coat and hair as I walk down to the site. I like the wind, though, and the way it pulls at me, like it's pleading with me to come play. There's a bounce in my step as I step onto the narrow lane that winds down to the valley's bottom.

Above me, the sky is a litter of stars, a glittering waste of them, and on the other side of the hill, I can see the lights of the fair, promising popcorn and cheap souvenirs and fun. Maybe Alfie and François have finally realized their Great French Love Affair awaits; maybe some of the others have paired off too.

The idea makes me happy. As a girl, I used to line up my Barbies and matchmake them until every doll was joined with another, endowing them with backstories long enough to justify entire seasons of a TV show, rewarding them with outrageous weddings and lavish honeymoons in my backyard. In high school, I spent a not insignificant amount of time helping my friends get within kissing range of the people they wanted to kiss—rivaled only by the amount of time I spent trying to get *myself* within kissing range of the people I wanted to kiss.

I craved romance and sex, yes, but more than that, I craved *happenings*. Novelty. I wanted everyone to be looking for love *or* falling in love *or* having their heart broken...I wanted everyone to be poised on the edge of some new cliff, ready to tumble into the next pool of excitement or pain.

My undergraduate years were when I learned that my appetite for—well, for *anything*—food, drinks, sex, parties— only grew deeper with the slaking. *Insatiable* is a word we throw around lightly, but it's more than a word for me. It's the very signature of my being, my mind, my belly.

Janneth Carter: insatiable.

And it's why despite many valiant forays into kink, polyamory, and hookup apps, I'm the one tramping alone through wet heather while everyone else is up at a fair stealing kisses and having fun.

Okay, that's not *really* true. I'm here because our work matters too much to let kids drunk on Buckfast stumble through uncovered dig pits...but it still feels true *emotionally*. I've learned the hard way that insatiable girls don't get happily ever afters. They eat their way through lovers and friends too heartily—and that they *also* want to be eaten alive, their blood drunk and their bones cracked open, is irrelevant.

Insatiable girls stay alone. Insatiable girls settle for living by proxy, for craving and wanting and shoving those wants down where they won't scare anyone away.

At least I have archaeology, an even hungrier lover than I am, beckoning with its long hours, its endless questions, its byzantine politics of publishing and funding and permissions.

And you know what? I have more than that. I have amazing friends and the plucking night wind and the stars and now the slow mist creeping over the dig site from the loch, wreathing the bent trees nearby and whispering at the base of the tomb. A pretty Halloween picture, just for me.

When I finally pick my way to the mouth of the cairn, the Halloween picture completes itself, because the lights *are* fire —torches stuck right into the soft earth around the turf-covered mound that makes up the ancient grave. The torches are as tall as I am and spaced so regularly that whoever planted them must've measured the gaps down to the half inch.

But there is no one here, no one at all.

No youths, no superstitious locals, no neopagans or tripod-toting influencers. Someone came to the middle of nowhere, made a ring of burning torches, and then just...left.

No. No, that can't be right. I don't even bother flicking on the bathroom light when I brush my teeth at night—who would go to all the trouble of carrying, planting, and then lighting torches just to leave?

They must still be here.

Squaring my shoulders and practicing my best teaching assistant voice in my head, I raise my phone flashlight and start circling the tomb. The word *tomb* or *cairn* gives a sense of smallness, maybe, a sense of containment relating to its purpose of holding one or a handful of bodies, but this cairn is nearly a hill all on its own on the valley floor, connected only at the very back to the hill that walls off the south side of the valley. The mound is taller than I am by several orders and wide enough that it takes me the better part of several minutes to check around its perimeter.

I'm still alone after I do.

Baffled, I return to the dig site itself, which is chiefly arrayed on the flat strip of land in front of the cairn and crenelated with plastic totes and heaped bags of sand. Tarps waiting to cover the pits ruffle a little, but the breeze down here is so gentle and still that it's nothing more than a sporadic flutter. Even the mist continues with its slow, unbothered swirls, following its own laws of physics as it moves between my legs and fills the low stone doorway of the cairn.

My headlamp's beam moves over the mist-veiled shore of the loch and over the dark water beyond, but there's nothing. No movement, no sound.

There really is no one here.

On the bright side, this means I can go to the fair now, which has me humming as I turn back to douse the torches before I leave, and then I see a shape standing directly in front of the tomb's entrance.

I bite off a yelp and drop my phone. My headlamp battery dies at the same moment.

The figure—illuminated now only by torchlight and moonlight—steps forward. Boots, jeans, peacoat, stylish wool beanie. Their gloves have reflective stitching on the forefingers and thumbs. The kind of gloves you wear so you can still use your phone while you're wearing them. Sensible, forethought-requiring gloves.

My pounding heart slows a little. It's just a person. Just a non–serial killer person.

Probably.

"It's dangerous to be out when the lights are lit," the stranger says, his voice deep and burred, although something about the cadence of his voice doesn't sound entirely Scottish to me. "Especially on this night, of all nights."

I squat and start patting for my phone. The lack of head-lamp and the picturesque-but-inconvenient mist makes it hard to see exactly where it fell—there is only the sight of my hands, pale in the darkness, sinking into the mist and then disap-pearing.

"Yes," I say, palpating the ground like I'm Aragorn looking for hobbit tracks. "Um. About that. See, this is actually an ongoing excavation—" My fingers brush against the sleek shape of my phone, and relieved, I grab it and stand. Which is when I realize the stranger has moved even closer—silently. He's now only a few paces away, and I can make out his pale, carved features and his eyes shining in the dark. They almost look like they reflect the moonlight, like a cat's, but then he looks back toward the cairn and the illusion vanishes. It must have been my imagination.

I clear my throat and start again. "You see, we're not finished securing the site for winter, and so it's not really ready for visitors—"

"Are you telling me to leave?" the stranger asks, amusement plain in his voice. "*I* must leave *here*?"

When I'm not on a dig site, I'm teaching moody undergraduates, so I'm used to batting away defiance and unearned condescension.

"That's right," I say firmly. "In the interest of conservation, we need to keep the site as clear as—"

"Oh, how *adorable*," comes a purring voice from behind the man. A woman with deep umber skin and hair the color of steel is approaching us—from the tomb, maybe?—and like the stranger, she is also wearing very normal clothes. Boots, jeans, coat. A scarf embroidered with silver butterfly-like shapes wound around her long neck. Despite her iron-colored hair, she looks to be my age. Maybe even younger. "She's perfect, Maynard."

I like being called perfect by a pretty woman as much as the next person, and I don't even mind being called adorable, since I've made something of a sexual career out of being short and curvy and dimple-cheeked.

But. Being pretty doesn't mean one floats over the ground when they walk; these people still can't be traipsing all over as-yet-unstabilized Bronze and Iron Age ruins.

I try a different tack. "I know you've probably come a long way to be here tonight, and I really am sorry to ask you to leave."

"We came from forever and a daydream away," the woman says, smiling.

The man—Maynard—shakes his head. "We came from only a whisper away. From a thought away."

"Both things are true," says the woman, stepping even closer. "All things are true."

"One thing *isn't* true," I say, the first tendrils of real exasperation strangling my good mood, "and it's that you can walk on an active dig site."

"Aren't you going to ask us which ones?" Maynard asks, ignoring me.

I stare. Firelight flickers behind him, and I see a new shadow. So now there are three people I have to shoo off. Fantastic.

"Which ones?" I echo distractedly. I'm following the movements of the new person and trying to think of what I can say to make them leave. They don't seem drunk, but maybe that's worse...

"Aren't you going to ask which whisper?" Maynard says in a silky murmur. "Which thought?"

His words from just a moment ago come back to me.

We came from only a whisper away. From only a thought away.

Maybe they *are* drunk, or he is, at least, and the thought is almost comforting. Drunkenness I can work with.

"I'll ask you which whisper if you walk me up to the fair over the hill," I say in my best *let's go have an adventure* voice. "They've got drinks and food up there and everything."

"A bargain!" says the woman delightedly. "She wants to make a bargain!"

"As if she could," the third stranger says. His voice is sneering, cold, and what I can see of his face in the torchlight is beautiful and severe. "She has nothing we want."

"She has something the queen wants," Maynard says, not taking his eyes from me.

My mind is filled with corgis and boxy handbags for a moment. "The queen?"

"It was fortunate we came upon you here," Maynard says as if I hadn't spoken. "We thought we might have to go to the Shadow Market to find you, but here you are, right at the mouth of hell. You would have wandered in all on your own, wouldn't you?"

"Just take her, Maynard," the woman says. Her face is pitying as she looks at me. "If she's not brought in tonight, the tithe might fail, and if the tithe fails, we will all pay the price."

"Speak for yourself, Idalia," the cold stranger says.

"I only ever do, *Your Highness*," Idalia rejoins, her voice on the furthest edge of what could be called polite.

I am still stuck on *just take her*.

"Okay, wait," I say, shoving my phone in my coat pocket so I can have both hands free. I hear the crinkle of a paper wrapper as I do—one of those eco-friendly bamboo cutlery sets that came with some long-ago takeaway lunch, crammed into my pocket and promptly forgotten.

I lift both my hands in front of me, like I'm talking to a drunk girl in a club bathroom who's just puked all over her dress. It's my *okay, okay, we can figure this out* stance. "You don't need to take anyone anywhere."

"And yet we do," the cold one says.

Idalia makes a regretful noise. "He's right, poppet."

"And for whatever opaque reason she has, it must be *you*," the cold one says. "No one else."

"S-she?"

No one else?

"He means the queen," Maynard says, and how his deep purr can sound both helpful and ominous, I have no idea. But

I do know he's close enough to touch me now, and that abruptly feels too close, far too close.

I try to step back and end up stumbling over part of a tarp as I do. It's what gets me in the end, that fucking tarp, because in my windmilling efforts to catch my balance, its layers slide over one another, and I'm falling back—

Maynard catches me. Hard hands on my biceps, effortless strength.

"The bard is gallant tonight," the cold one says, and this must be some joke at Maynard's expense, because Maynard's mouth—dramatically full in the middle, even more dramatically thin at the corners—flattens into a line. But his eyes remain on my face.

"Come with us, Janneth, and you will have every wish fulfilled. Come, and you'll know not hunger nor cold nor the stale kiss of death. I will sing to you of your own whispers and your own thoughts; I will croon to you of secrets untold for lifetimes. And you will know the taste of your own longing only as a garnish, not as its own meal, for in our world, there is only ever surfeit, never any lack."

I blink up at him. His grip on my arms isn't painful, but its close enough to it that adrenaline still doses my blood. I realize the metallic taste in my mouth is fear.

"How do you know my name?" I ask shakily.

"That question will be answered, and many others, if you come with me now."

I feel like I can't keep hold of my own thoughts. "Come with you where?"

"To the court of the queen," Maynard responds, as if there's no other place.

And that's when I decide to cut my losses. The site will just have to be trampled and god knows what else because these people aren't going to leave on my account, and I have no interest in going anywhere with them that's not a bright public place like the fair to lure them away. In fact, they sound an awful lot like *they're* the ones doing the luring, and yes, I've done some dicey shit in my life in the name of having a good time, but this really feels like a line not to cross.

Even *I* have lines, apparently! That's kind of reassuring because sometimes I worry I don't. But following three strangers to *the court of the queen* in the fullness of night screams BAD IDEA, even to me.

"No, thank you?" I offer.

Idalia clucks sympathetically, like she's just watched a bird fly into a window.

"A shame," Maynard says. "Then you have my apologies."

"Apologies for what—"

It's too late. Idalia and the cold one are close, on top of me —and a blindfold is wrapped around my head from behind— and I'm fighting—and then the blindfold is tied tight, and my wrists are bound. I struggle and push, but it doesn't matter because these strangers are the kind of strong that defies human biology. It's like trying to ram my shoulder against a rock, like trying to unpin myself from a fallen tree.

I'm trapped and I'm theirs, and now they will take me wherever they want.

I scream, and my scream pierces the valley. Faintly, over the sound of the waves lapping at the loch's shore, I hear a rising trill of screams coming from the far side of the hill, chased by the sound of calliope music, frenetic and bright. My scream dies away as it sinks in: no one is at the farmhouse, and no one at the fair will hear me over their own shrieks of delight, over the music that promises big smiles and light pockets.

"There now, poppet," Idalia says. "Save some of your screams for the queen, there's a good girl."

And then I'm slung over a shoulder and carried away from the shore and the dig site and any sliver of safety I might have had.

CHAPTER 3

After a moment, the person carrying me ducks, and then the air becomes still and close and the world smells of old wet stone.

I stop struggling as he—I think it's Maynard—straightens back up. I'm certain we're inside the cairn itself, and I rack my brain for any way to use that to my advantage and come up dry. The inside of the cairn was empty when we started our excavation outside, long ago robbed of its bones and grave goods, and so there's nothing in here remotely resembling a weapon. Nothing but earthen floor and chambered ceiling large enough to rival that of Maeshowe in Orkney.

My headlamp slides off my head and falls to the packed earth with a small *thud*.

Before I can wonder why they've brought me inside a tomb and consider how sinister a move that might be, Maynard ducks once more, and then I feel breeze and mist-kissed air, and the world smells again of autumn, turning, dying.

Back outside.

"Please," I say. The word is practically a wheeze—I'm not

a small woman, and being slung over someone's shoulder like this has driven all the air right out of me. "Please, let me go. I won't tell anyone, I swear."

"A vow from a mortal means very little," the cold one says.

"It doesn't matter, Morven," Idalia says, seeming a little irritated at his bad attitude. "There's no one she could tell who would believe her. How many mortals have gone back to their world singing songs and telling tales?"

I don't like all this *mortal* talk. Because—well, look: after spending the past six years dissecting medieval narratives about demons and witches, I'm hardly one to jump into Satanic Panic mode, but there are a *lot* of the right ingredients here. I'm being carried off from a pagan tomb on Halloween night by attractive but possibly sociopathic strangers, and they're talking about queens and mortals, and *oh god*—I'm going to die, I'm really going to die, and it's not even going to be while I'm having an irresponsible but murder-podcast-worthy good time...

I struggle on Maynard's shoulder, trying to shove off my blindfold with my bound hands, but I'm given a hard, impatient spank for my efforts. *Spanked*. Like we're playing naughty French maids or something.

And I like playing a naughty French maid game as much as the next pervy grad student—particularly if there's spanking involved—and I'm not saying I *haven't* occasionally dreamed of being kidnapped and tortured with sexy shit—but this isn't a dream, this is my real-ass Halloween night.

"Are you going to squirm the whole time?" Maynard asks.

"You won't notice me squirming if you put me down," I suggest helpfully.

"But then you'll run," Maynard says, as if he's explaining something to me instead of the other way around. "No matter. The way to the queen is not long. In the right conditions, at least."

"I don't know what that means," I say. I try squirming again, but all I get is another swat, and a tug on my hair from Idalia.

"It means there is a shortcut. The castle could be merely a question away instead of a few hours' walk away," Idalia informs me. "But it must be a true question, a curiosity. Burning in the mind like the tongue of a flame."

I squeeze my eyes closed behind my blindfold because I might start crying if I don't. Nothing they're saying makes any sense at all, and I can't even begin to imagine where they're taking me. I'm fairly sure we're not heading *toward* the fair, given that I hear nothing more of the screams or music, but I also don't think we're near the loch any longer because I don't hear the slow lick of the waves on the shore. I hear—well, it almost sounds like *forest* noises: leaves underfoot, branches creaking, an owl *hoo*-ing out a warning.

But there aren't any wooded areas near the dig—not any properly wooded ones, anyway. There is a string of weary trees near the farmhouse and a few ancient ones near the site, and then a thin seam of woods two valleys over. But that valley is three miles away and impossible to make by foot with the steepness of the hills. Even the sheep have trouble getting over those hills, and sheep are dicks who like nothing more than to find places where they're certain to die horribly.

And more than that, there's nothing that can be remotely called a castle within ten miles of here, which I know, obviously, because the whole point of this dig was to find out where de Segovia had stayed after that fateful storm.

Wait.

Castle.

Maybe they know something I don't? What if the castle survived—or its ruins survived—somewhere nearby? What if Dr. Siska got the location wrong after all?

"Ah, there it is," Idalia says, and Maynard answers with a

low melodious hum. "Well done," she tells me, with a pat on my shoulder that feels almost fond. "I knew you'd get us there faster."

I twist enough to tug again at my blindfold, and this time the others let me, Maynard still humming and someone playfully kicking the leaves as they walk. The first thing I see when the blindfold drops to the ground is a flutter of dark velvet. A pair of gleaming riding boots. Then—flying bugs.

Moths. Softly furred, bone-white in the moonlight.

The blood has gone to my head, I think, because when I look up, the moths are fluttering around Idalia, clustering in a thick wreath around her neck, like a scarf. No, not like a scarf, but *as* a scarf, because the scarf she was wearing earlier is gone, and there is nothing but moths, their wings beating, their antennae moving in the night air.

And then Maynard sets me on my feet—roughly but not cruelly—and I sway a moment as the blood returns to the rest of my body. I close my eyes as I do, hoping that when I open them again, I'll see something I recognize. A car park, a farmer rounding up a stray ewe, a Tesco, *something.* But no.

There is Idalia with her ruff of moths, and there is Maynard, wearing not jeans and boots but a velvet cape, breeches, and riding boots. Morven is in much the same, although his clothes are a deep sable compared to Maynard's crimson and buff.

I stare at them. They can't have changed while we were walking, right? At least Maynard couldn't have—so it follows that I must have been wrong about what they were wearing before, at the site. I must have...imagined...Maynard's tech-friendly gloves, Idalia's embroidered scarf...

Maynard puts his hands on my shoulders and turns me, firmly, until I'm facing the opposite direction. Until I'm facing the spires and ramparts of a castle.

An impossible castle.

There are no castles like this in Scotland. Anything this turreted and graceful would be a nineteenth-century confection, made for leisure and not for defense, and yet this was unmistakably also built with defense in mind. The deep moat, the imposing barbican. The thick walls buttressed with sloped taluses and punctured with arrow slits.

And it seems to be formed entirely out of the hill it sits upon. Not fitted together with stone, not even *built* so much as carved out of the living hill itself, as if chewed into existence by Sir Walter Scott–reading termites: grass and earth and rock at the bottom; sheer, fog-wetted stone at the top.

Lights glow from within; torches flicker on the walls.

"Come," Idalia says, nudging my shoulder with hers. Moths flutter around my face and tickle my jaw. "The queen is waiting."

THE INSIDE of the castle is even stranger than the outside, and even though I know in a distant sort of way that this is my moment for escape, my curiosity is like a leash yanking me ever forward. My feet drag as the trio lead me over bridges, and through doorways, and into the massive keep itself, and I can't stop swiveling my head from one side to the other, trying to drink it all in.

The floors of the castle are flagged—except when they're tiled in elaborate mosaics, and even then, half the mosaics aren't tile at all but gleaming bits of petrified wood and gemstones. Some halls are carpeted in living grass—growing as lushly as it might outside—dotted with small wildflowers. Some of the walls are made not of stone but of curtains of falling water, and some are made of mist, trapped in place like vapor between panes of invisible glass.

There are carvings, paintings hung from sturdy rails, tapestries depicting battles and hunts. Busts sit in niches, and mushrooms bloom in corners and give off a faint silver light too dim to rival the glow of the torches and candelabra but bright enough to cast strange shadows where the firelight can't reach.

I can't absorb it all—there's too much—and just that, just the thought that there's *too much*, speeds my heart. I could spend days and weeks in one hallway and not even come close to finding every detail, studying every carving, exploring every corner. We pass rooms upon rooms, halls upon halls—some crowded with more people like Maynard and Idalia, beautiful and strange, and some so eerily empty and cobwebbed that they look as if they've been untouched for centuries.

It feels like hours, but eventually we make our way to two doors made of gray-green wood and carved into twists of ivy, and Maynard knocks once.

A woman's voice calls from within. "Intrare."

He opens one of the doors and, with a hand firm on my elbow, guides me inside the high-ceilinged room. Bookshelves line the walls, going up one story and then another, the very top recesses disappearing into shadow. Chandeliers hang from the ceiling, but there are mushrooms set into their holders instead of candles, tall and skinny and glowing silver. Threads of luminous mycelium wind up their chains, until they too disappear into the darkness above. The only other light comes from glassed sconces mounted on the wall, lamps that burn steadily and almost solemnly, if solemn burning is a thing. They are blue, rather than orange and yellow, sapphire at their cores and a pale sky color at their tips.

I stare open-mouthed as Maynard hauls me forward and Morven stalks behind us. Idalia's moths flit in front of my face as I take in the sheer number of texts here—ancient-looking scrolls, tomes thick with wavy vellum pages, books chained to their shelves with fetters made of silver and gleaming gold.

I'm so entranced by the books I don't realize we're walking toward someone at the front of the room until we stop right in front of her. Maynard pulls on my elbow—hard—and I tumble right to my knees, which must be what he wanted me to do, because he steps back and then kneels himself, pressing his hand to his heart. Idalia does the same the next to me, as does Morven, although a bit more bitterly.

I bow my head like they do, having only gotten a glimpse of dark hair and ivory-pale skin. She wears a dress long enough to puddle around her feet on the stone floor of the room, and it's a red so deep it looks black in its folds and creases. A silk so shiny that I wonder if it's wet. I stare at the hem as she speaks.

Her voice is low and musical, lilted the same as the others', rich in a way that's intoxicating to hear. Like each of her words is a sip of a sweet ruby liqueur. "And there was no trouble?"

"None, Your Majesty," Idalia says.

"Good. The banquet will begin soon, then. You should be ready."

"Yes, Your Majesty."

When I hear them rise behind me, the woman speaks again. "Morven, please wait outside the doors. You will be needed before you can make yourself ready."

Morven's displeasure radiates so palpably through the space that I can sense it even with my back to him and my eyes on the hem of the woman's dress.

"Yes, Your Majesty," he answers stiffly, and then I hear him leave after the others.

After the door closes, we are alone.

"Look at me," the woman says, and curiosity still burning brighter than any other feeling, I obey.

CHAPTER 4

Even without the thin circle of gold set in her hair, there is something about her bearing, something about her expression...It reminds me of the way cats sit and stags stand. It reminds me of the unhurried way the moon skims across the sky. There is a completeness about her, a certainty, and a well of power that isn't interested in proving itself, since such a thing would be unnecessary. Redundant. It speaks for itself.

She speaks for herself.

The queen is not beautiful in the usual way, but she *is* beautiful, of that there is no doubt. High cheekbones, brows in dark arches. Her eyes, blacker than the spaces between stars. A mouth with a full lower lip and then a sharply peaked upper lip. Those lips are painted a dark red, but they seem to be the only ornamented part of her face, for the lashes fanning thickly from her eyes need no assistance, and neither does her skin, which is smooth, save for two faint lines bracketing her mouth. I could call them smile lines, but I won't, because it is hard to imagine her smiling often enough to cause them.

The queen's jaw is squared and precise, and her nose is

long and bumped at the bridge, and when it's all put together, the strong, dramatic features and the coal-black eyes, she's impossible to look at and impossible to look away from.

I am suddenly very grateful to Maynard for forcing me to my knees.

"Welcome to my castle," the queen says finally. "Have you seen anything like it?"

I've never been in a room lit by mushrooms and walled with chained books, nor have I been in a castle carved entirely from earth and bedrock, nor I have I ever been kidnapped on Halloween night. And I don't think I've ever seen anyone like her, whose face I could look at for the rest of my life and still need to look at longer.

"This is a dream," I say, sounding more dazed than certain.

"All things are dreams," the queen says, voice as cool and impersonal as the walls made of falling water outside this room.

"How can I wake up?"

"You cannot," the queen says. "There is no waking from this. There is only this and the dream you came from, nothing else."

I swallow, dropping my eyes back to the hem of her dress. I want to wake up. I want to be at the fair with Alfie and the others; I want to be in my bed at the farmhouse, counting the hours until I'm back in Edinburgh and my hookup apps pull up more than the *no results in search radius* message I get out in these parts.

"Why am I here?" I whisper.

"Do you even know where *here* is?" the queen asks.

"I guess not." Maybe if it isn't a dream...maybe if I'm still awake and this is real, then *here* matters. Because if this is truly the castle de Segovia stumbled upon, then I need to know how I got here and how to get back. How to bring others here, maybe.

25

How to bring others to the castle made of mist and mush-rooms? Yeah, right, Janneth. This place can't be real.

"This is the Court of Stags," the queen says. "In Elphame, which is called Faerie by most."

Elphame is a word I know plenty well, between a fun semester gamboling with Thomas the Rhymer and several weeks' worth of late nights poring over records of the Scottish witch trials for a paper. And even though my focus is on the medieval *archaeological* record, I'm enough of a former fairy stan that I soaked up every fairy mention I found in my research. And you know what? Okay, between Elphame and the castle, I think I've got to be dreaming. I just listened to a great audiobook about mushrooms and fungus last week, and I was rereading de Segovia's journal, and maybe I fell asleep on the bed. And I'm so tired and rumpled and chronically sex deprived that I'm having a weird, super-active dream about Elphame and mushrooms and a hot, scary queen.

The queen's fingers find my chin, and she tilts my face up to hers. "You don't seem surprised."

"Faerie isn't real," I tell the fairy queen. "So I know this must be a dream."

She lifts a silk-clad shoulder in a shrug. What Janneth Carter considers to be reality and unreality doesn't seem very important to her.

"What happens now?" I ask. Even in a dream, it feels important to know.

"You are a guest here," she says. "And as such, you are permitted any freedom you'd like, save for one."

I'd be a fool not to ask. "And what is that?"

Her fingers tighten on my jaw. "The freedom to leave."

I blink up at her. Her expression betrays nothing, gives me nothing, save for this: she means it.

I am not to leave here. Or her.

There's a strange curl in my chest at the thought.

"And how long must I stay?" I ask.

"Two nights," the queen pronounces. One finger traces along my jaw, and then she releases me. "And on the third, you can leave Faerie."

She does not elaborate on the last part.

"Two nights," I echo.

"And now there will be a feast in your honor," she says. "You will sit by my side, and drink from my cup, and together we will see what revels Faerie has to offer on Samhain night."

"And I'll be able to leave Faerie on the third night?" I ask to confirm. This is how they always get the unsuspecting high school heroines in the fan fictions—a twist of language, a trick of words.

"You will," allows the queen.

"And it won't be like a hundred years have passed or something? I won't go back and find out all my friends and family are dead?"

"Three days will feel different passed here than in your lands, but not that much different. One day here is longer than a day in yours."

A new fear takes hold. "Wait. Promise I won't be like a million years old when I go back."

There is a slight lift to her eyebrow now. "You're very preoccupied with this."

"You would be too if you were mortal," I mutter, and the eyebrow goes higher. I suppose I'm not being very respectful right now.

"You will leave Faerie the same age you entered it, plus only a handful of hours more. This I swear."

"If you say so," I say, and she runs her fingers across my jaw again. Her touch is warm and lingering. Her fingers move to my lips, and that curl in my chest twists lower.

"I do say so," she says, one fingertip making a slow line

over my lower lip, dragging over the place where the skin of my lip becomes smooth and damp.

I think it would be charming to claim that what happens next happens out of some resonant instinct, that I do it because I sense it would please her and I want to be pleasing—but the truth is more immediate than that, and much more selfish. I do it because I am greedy, and my greed very rarely listens to common sense or exigent circumstances like abduction.

I part my lips as she touches me. I open my mouth enough for her to see the pink of my tongue and the edges of my teeth. To show her she could push her fingers into my mouth if she'd like.

Because I'd like her to. Because even though I was kidnapped by someone named Maynard and carried to a mushroom castle, even though I'm so very certain this is a dream, it would be a very good mushroom castle dream if she put her fingers in my mouth.

Something moves in the queen's eyes then, but I can't say what it is—only that for an instant, the black irises seem darker than ever, less the spaces between stars and more whatever came before the stars kindled into being. I don't know if it's a good thing or a bad thing, but I do think I could sink into the inky well of her gaze and never resurface.

And then, as quickly as it came, it is gone, and her stare is as cool and remote as before.

"You will go with Morven," she says, her hand dropping from my face, "to make ready for the meal. He'll show you where you'll sleep as well."

She snaps her fingers, and the doors to the library swing open. Morven stands in the doorway, looking faintly pissed off. She doesn't speak to him, but he seems to know what she wants all the same. He jerks his head toward the hallway.

"Come, mortal girl," he says shortly. "We don't have much time."

THE CASTLE IS MOST DEFINITELY *MADE* and not formed —the floors are flat, the corners squared, and the spaces as lofty as any medieval hall—some maybe more so, although with ceilings that often vanish into darkness, it is impossible to tell. That said, the layout of the castle resists a feeling of architecture, or if it is architecture, it is meant to be an intricate tangle of it, a knot of passages, galleries, halls, and stairs. It feels more like the warren of a cave system than a palace, and I feel the hopeless crush of getting lost stealing over me, like I can't make sense of this place's shape or size or relationship with itself. And having cut my archaeological teeth on the cramped clutter of three medieval monasteries built on top of each other, that is saying something.

Morven, either oblivious to my disorientation, or more likely not giving a shit about it, walks quickly in front of me, his black cloak fluttering around his thighs as he does. Despite our so-fast-I-almost-need-to-jog pace, I'm able to study his features more closely than before and observe something that makes Morven's barely there deference to the queen make more sense. He also has a long nose, slightly bumped in the middle, and a sharp jaw, and even though he has moon-white hair instead of black, he has the same coal-dark eyes as the queen. Judging from his similarly unlined face, they must be around the same age: older than me but young enough to make that a guess rather than a certainty.

If they aren't brother and sister, then they're the kind of cousins who look like it.

"Here," Morven says as we come to a stop before another

ornately carved door. This one is carved with stags instead of ivy and, in the middle, the carved shape of a naked man with antlers twining from his head. "This is where you will sleep, if you sleep at all."

He opens the door and leads the way inside.

Though the walls are made from stone, there's something almost airy about the room. The ceiling is high and elaborately corbelled, the walls curve generously—perhaps even fondly—around the bed and furniture inside, and a window of leaded glass opens into the night. Outside, the moon hangs, red and ripe looking.

I walk over to the window and look out—and then down. I'm high up in a tower. A real castle tower, like for a damsel in a fairy tale.

This has to be a dream.

"You'll find clothes in the wardrobe," Morven says, still standing at the door. "Anything in there will be an improvement on what you're wearing now."

I look down at my clothes. Stained leather boots, ripstop pants, and a waterproof coat. Dig clothes, because I hadn't yet changed for going to the fair with the others. A little rough and ready maybe, but that's excavation life. Normally, I prefer to look very tweedy and academic, but I can't afford to dry-clean my *Mona Lisa Smile* cosplay every day on a dig, not on a grad student's income.

"I was working today," I say in my defense, but Morven doesn't seem to care.

"When you are ready to come down to the hall, follow the leaves on the floor." He turns to leave, and I'm suddenly gripped with a kind of panic.

"Do I have to go to this feast?" I plead. "Can't I just stay here?"

"You cannot stay in your room," he replies. "You—as am I—are bound to the queen's whims."

"She said I was a guest," I say. "That I was permitted freedoms. Any freedoms."

He steps forward, his eyes flashing. "Oh, did she tell you that? Did she tell you that you could do anything you liked except leave? You are her doll to pick up and throw down at will. You are a toy to be broken and then traded away when the time comes."

Those are very scary and very pretty words. Dream words. "But *why*?" I press.

He comes even closer, his strides long and graceful, and stops only a few paces away. His voice is quiet and silky when he speaks. "Are you asking why someone might want to have a toy, Janneth Carter? You who so like to be one?"

There's no way he can know that about me, no possible way. It's a wild guess—or he knows it because this is a dream and he is an extension of myself inside it.

"Why does she need a *new* toy, then?" I ask, refusing to let him intimidate me. "We're in a castle, and she's a queen. Surely she has an entire court of people to play with already."

He takes a step closer, and then another. The fire crackling in the stone fireplace limns his features in scarlet and turns his eyes the color of the sunrise. He reaches toward me, fingers long and elegant, and despite his hostility, despite his contempt, he is too beautiful to resist. I let him trace along my jaw and then drop his hand to the zipper of my coat.

Over the waterproof material, I feel his fingertips find the zipper tab, and then I feel as he slowly, deliberately, pulls it down. One plastic tooth, and then another, and then another, monstrously slow.

His mouth is a little fuller even than the queen's, and his eyes burn, and he is so gorgeous, so tall, and being tall shouldn't matter, but sometimes it does, especially if the tall person has their hand on your zipper, and I'm breathing harder than I should, my lips already parted, as if ready for a kiss.

He drops his hand abruptly, moving back, and I realize I've been leaning forward enough to nearly lose my balance. I step forward to catch myself, and he gives me a smile nearly dazzling in its cruelty.

"Because mortal toys are more fun," he says. "And more beloved. And when beloved things bleed, the land sings."

And with that final cryptic remark, he leaves me alone.

CHAPTER 5

I *should wake up.*
And if I'm awake, then I should leave.
Or I should stay and learn where the fuck I am.

There are good reasons to do any one of those things, but unfortunately, it's not a good reason that drives me forward to the wardrobe after Morven leaves. It's the memory of the queen's fingers on my mouth. It's wondering if her eyes are as dark as I remember.

I'll go down to the feast, *and then* I'll figure out what to do. That seems like a good enough plan for now.

And as much as it irritates me, Morven was telling the truth about the clothes. Everything in the wardrobe is much nicer than what I'm wearing now, even though it's all fantastical as hell—velvets and watered silks and brocades embroidered with gold and silver thread. They feel soft and silky to the touch as I run my fingers through them.

I have my doubts as I finally settle on a dress and start shucking off my dig clothes...my body is generous with its curves, and I have a hard enough time finding clothes that accommodate my tits and ass when I have an entire Internet to shop from. I'm not holding out hope that a random wardrobe in a random castle that shouldn't exist is well stocked with plus-sized court gowns.

Except, impossibly, the dress *does* fit. It fits perfectly, as if it were tailored for me.

A dream dress, Janneth. Obviously it fits.

I find a tall mirror next to the wardrobe and admire myself in the bronze light of the fire. The dress is made of layers and layers of blush-colored tulle, the outermost layer stitched with small gold and silver stars. They glimmer while I look, as if I'm wearing fabric scissored out of the night sky and stitched onto the first breath of dawn. The bodice is boned and laced with corset laces, which after stumping around Edinburgh as a living history tour guide during my undergrad years, I'm able to lace and tighten on my own without a problem. The sleeves are sheer and detached, leaving my shoulders bare, and there's a slit high in the skirt that exposes my leg when I move. You can see the tattoo on my thigh, the reds and golds of Frank Cadogan Cowper's *La Belle Dame sans Merci*, a woman sitting above a cursed knight, pinning her long red hair up as she looks down at his armored, cobwebbed form.

A tattoo from a different time, for a different Janneth. A version of myself that I'd long ago said goodbye to.

At the bottom of the wardrobe, I find a pair of silver slippers that pair well with the dress, and on the dressing table, I see a slender diadem made of golden stars. I brush my hair until it hangs in gleaming blonde waves and then set the diadem onto my head. It winks along with my nose ring.

Dressed, I open the door to the hallway and see a dusting of leaves on the stone floor. Bright orange and ruby leaves that weren't there when we were outside the room just half an hour ago. When I step, the leaves drift in a lazy swirl forward, beckoning me onward like a variegated GPS.

Follow the leaves.

It's cool outside the tower, and I decide to grab my coat. The boxy, polyester thing is hardly court appropriate, but since I have *a lot of doubts* about how much that matters, I take it anyway. But I feel stupid carrying it, and I've only made it a few doors down the hallway angling off from my tower when I stop and try to think rationally about all this. Rational thinking is something insatiable girls have to learn at some point, and I'd had to learn it after I bought myself a one-way ticket from Kansas to come study abroad in Scotland and then spent months living on coffee, cereal, and leftover pastries from faculty meetings.

I'd especially had to learn it after the first semester of archaeology classes, when professors started tearing apart my fantasies of what archaeology would be, dusting off my imaginings, and showing the broken shards of my ideas for what they were: cracked, dime-a-dozen detritus.

Rational thinking or not, it takes me physically holding my coat to realize something I've forgotten, which is *my phone*, and I dig into my coat pocket to pull it out. It lights up right away, but as I'm opening my text messages, I realize I have no signal. Not even the gleam in a cell tower's eye of a signal. Not unusual for this part of the Highlands, but sometimes if you're on the right hill and the wind is southerly and the clouds are parted, you can catch a stray whiff of it long enough to check your email.

But not in the hot lady's mushroom castle apparently.

I've stopped in front of a tall, mullioned window, one of its sides open to the night air. The leaves shiver fretfully around my feet, as if anxious about my pause in forward motion, but I ignore the magic leaves and turn my phone off and then back on again.

It doesn't matter. Still no bars. And my battery is low, which probably also isn't ideal.

I put my phone back in my pocket, and I have a moment

when I think about how easy it would be to step on the ledge and then jump down to the moat below. It's not an easy fall—maybe not even a safe fall—but I might be willing to sprain an ankle in the name of getting out of here. And if all this *is* a strange kind of dream, well, then falls are supposed to wake you up from dreams. I saw that in a movie once.

"It is a long way down to the water," someone says from behind me, and it takes me a moment to process what they've said, not because it isn't true—it's patently true—but because they haven't spoken in English.

Longum iter est usque ad aquam.

Latin.

Most legal and ecclesiastical documents from medieval Scotland were written in Latin, which means knowledge of Latin is something of a necessity in my area of research. But I haven't heard it *spoken* very much since my undergrad studies —I read the stuff, but I don't converse in it at the pub or anything.

I turn and face the person who spoke. He doesn't have a ruff of moths or impossible eyes. He's a pale, middle-aged man with grave features and a dark beard. Like the others I've seen, he's wearing a cloak, but unlike the others, he's in a doublet and trunk hose, all black and silver, looking like he's stepped out of a portrait from Holbein's emo phase.

"It is a long way down," I say, my own Latin coming out halting and imperfectly conjugated. Then I have a thought—well, the seed of a thought, anyway. "Is there any way you can help me?"

"It would be my honor," he says. "I expect you need help making it to the queen's hall?"

"No," I say quickly. "Can you help me leave? Can you help me get out of the castle?"

He gives me a pitying look. "There's no leaving unless the queen allows it."

I take in his strange clothes again, think about his Latin. "Not even for you?"

"My leaving would be...complicated," he says, but doesn't seem inclined to offer any more information than that.

I try again, still in Latin. Fuck, I wish I'd joined that Latin club at my university now, they have their meetings at a wine bar and everything. "If the queen doesn't *allow* us to leave, then the only way to leave is by escaping. So...can you help me escape?"

"I've sworn to the antlered crown never to help a fellow mortal do any act that would displease a monarch of Elphame," he tells me, utterly seriously.

I stare at him. "Well, can you...*un*swear...it?"

To his credit, he does look very regretful when he says, "I cannot. A vow to a crown of Elphame can only be forsworn at great cost."

I close my eyes and sigh. "Maybe this is still a dream and it doesn't matter."

I feel him take my hand, and I open my eyes. The regret hasn't left his face when he says, "This isn't a dream, child."

"This has to be a dream. A castle like this—*fairies*—" I don't know the actual Latin word for fairies, so I settle for *daemones.* "It can't be real."

He pinches the top of my hand, and I yelp, yanking it out of his grip. "I promise you, this place is real, and you are awake," he says. "You will be able to feel, taste...read...things we cannot do properly in dreams."

I rub the skin on the top of my hand, bothered more than I can say.

"Please believe me," the man says. "Please accept this. Your life will depend on it."

"My life? *What*? Why?" I ask.

The leaves stir again at my feet, like an alarm going off to remind me I'm supposed to be moving.

"We must go down to the banquet," the man says, offering me his arm. "It will not be good if you are missed."

I don't move to take his arm.

"I promise to answer any questions you might have—questions I am permitted to answer—on the way to the banquet. But please, we must go there now, or else we risk the queen's anger."

"Is that such a bad thing?" I grumble, but I take the man's arm. The leaves around our feet give a hopeful flutter.

"It is worse than you can imagine," the man says grimly.

The leaves skate along the floor in front of us as we begin walking, but the man doesn't seem to need them. Much. There is a time early on when he and the leaves seem to disagree about which set of stairs to take; after wandering down an unlit corridor lined with brambles for a few moments, it becomes clear we should have listened to the leaves.

The leaves seem to know this too, because there's something almost smug about the way they find us and lead us back to the right set of stairs.

"Okay," I say and then remember my Latin. "So why will my life depend on my knowing this is real?"

The man seems to be thinking about what to say, and I recall the way he phrased his earlier offer. *Questions I am permitted to answer.* "The Court of Stags is one of the oldest courts in Elphame, and perhaps the proudest. They do not think much of mortals, and they do not think of violence and death the same way we do. You must be careful, watchful, and clever. You must not drift from pleasure to pleasure or from pain to pain. You *must* have intention with everything you do."

"Or?"

"Or they will hurt you or hunt you or kill you. Death is very much like life to them, and the reverse is also true."

This fairy abduction experience isn't shaping up to be very awesome for me. "And you will not help me escape?"

"I *cannot*," he corrects.

"And your advice is what then? To be...wary?"

"Wariness can get you far," he says. "I've been in at the Stag Court for over four hundred years, and I'm yet alive."

I look over at him. His style of clothing certainly speaks to a long-ago time, but then again, so does the clothing of everyone else here. And I've been in archaeology long enough to know that *four hundred years old* doesn't typically express as a carefully groomed beard and a few wrinkles in the forehead. *Four hundred years old* looks like dry bones with some bits of hair and clothing left.

"You said I was a fellow mortal earlier," I say. We turn the corner into a large, empty hall, and the leaves dance farther and farther ahead of us, as if impatient. At the end of the hall, I see a set of large double doors, made of wood but covered in the pale beams and tines of antlers. They are closed, but light glows from underneath. "Meaning you are mortal too?"

"Yes," the man says. "And no. And yes. As I said before, it is complicated."

I can hear music as we get closer to the doors, smell the inviting scent of roasted meat and sweet, flaky things.

"Now," the man says, stopping us and taking both my hands. "There is much that I cannot say because of the vows I made long ago. But three things I am not forbidden from telling you, so please heed them well."

I'm feeling a little disoriented from the whole *this is real, fairies don't sweat murder, this man is four hundred years old* spiel, but I try to make my best heeding face. It must work, because he continues. "Firstly, words have an effect here that they do not in our world. And that is not a figurative statement—in Elphame, speech can shape the earth, it can summon destinies. For the people born here, language is different. Vows can only be broken with great pain, if at all, and lies can never be told."

"Okay, okay, no lying," I say, and even though the *okay*s are in English, the man must get my meaning, because he gently shakes my hand.

"You are not listening. It is not that fairies should not tell lies, it is that they *cannot* tell them. Everything they speak, they must believe to be true. You are freed of that, being mortal and with mortal salt still in your blood, but I would still not lie here, not unless you absolutely must. The folk detest it."

"Mortal salt in my blood?" I ask. I know that's probably not the most important part of what he just said, but it is the creepiest.

He nods, as if he wanted me to ask exactly that. "You carry in your body the memory of the place you came from, but that flesh-and-bone memory will fade over time, and when it does, you will be bound to the land here and you will not be able to return. Or if you return, that return must be bought at great cost. But consuming salt from our world will forestall this process. So long as you salt your food here with mortal salt, you will be able to return."

"So I just need to find...salt from my world. Here."

"There will be containers on every table filled with mortal salt," my guide tells me. "A long-ago monarch of this court made a vow of salt hospitality at his table. But like most things in Elphame, you'll find there are some important caveats. Salt is only present at meals, and it is only *provided*, not offered. You must take it yourself, and you must be on guard against those who might convince you to eat food without it. A few bites, a few meals even, without it, and you might be safe. *Might* be. It is better not to risk it."

I exhale. "So no lying, and eat mortal salt whenever I can. Is there anything else?"

The man casts a look at the antler-covered door, and a

strange expression moves over his face. He opens his mouth again, abruptly swallows, and then clears his throat. "There is one other thing that I would have you hear. You should not feel safe."

I think of the salt and the *death is very much like life to them*, and also of Morven's little *mortal toys are more fun* comment. "Feeling safe is not going to be a problem," I mutter.

He shakes my hands again. "Please listen. The folk here love a bargain above all else; they love *price*. One thing for another. You might be able to buy some safety that way."

"But the queen said I could leave Elphame in three days! Are you really suggesting that something bad could happen to me in three days?" I pause, listening to what I've just said. Thinking back to the queen's words in the library.

Realizing the deal I struck might not be as solid as I thought.

"There is safety in being desired," he says. "If you wish no harm to come to you until you leave Elphame, it's something to consider." He looks at the doors again, and he looks at them not as if he's thinking of room on the other side of them, but as if he's looking at the doors themselves. The antlers, I realize. He's looking at the antlers. "The queen is the most powerful person here."

"And so she is the safest?"

He gives me a sharp look. "I did not say that. You must never confuse power and safety, not *ever*—and especially not in Elphame."

He looks very much like he wants to shake me again—not just my hands this time but my entire body—until it's clear that I understand.

"I won't, I won't, I promise," I tell him, and he gives me a quick nod.

"We will go in now. You will be expected to sit by the

queen. You would do well to please her—and don't forget the salt."

He takes a step toward the door, and I follow, but I pull on his hands. "Wait, you didn't tell me your name!" I say. "I'm Janneth."

He heaves a giant sigh, and considering how serious he is, it's almost funny to see him look so put out by such a small request.

"You should know that names have power here, true and full names at least. Not over you, not yet, but for those of us without mortal salt in our blood." He looks at me and seems to come to a decision. "Don Felipe de Moncada y Gralla," he says in a low voice. "That is my full name."

"Thank you, Felipe."

He sighs again, like I truly tax him so, and presses his hand to the antlered door. It swings open in front of us.

It's only as we step forward that my brain conjures up helpful information: I've heard Felipe's name before. In the photocopied account that's currently tossed haphazardly on a bed in a rural Scottish farmhouse. Felipe was—*is*—one of the missing companions of Hugo de Segovia. One of the companions who didn't return from the castle of silver and mist.

Which means that if I had any doubt before, I can erase it now. This is the same place.

Hugo de Segovia and his fellow shipwrecked sailors somehow found their way into the heart of fairyland.

CHAPTER 6

I don't have long to digest this, however, because the scene in front of me is a tangle of wild indulgence, and I'm not even sure how I'm supposed to make my way through it.

The hall is lofty, although its recesses doesn't disappear into darkness like so many ceilings do here. Instead, I can see it high above us, ribbed with hammer beams, rafters, braces. Each hammer beam is carved with the figure of a running stag so that it looks as if the entire roof of the castle rests on their cobwebbed backs. Just as in the library, threads of mycelium twist around the rafters and the chains of the chandeliers, glowing a pale silver in the gloom.

The walls are made of dark wood but are covered in living heather and gorse, the gorse blown butter yellow with red and orange leaves caught among its thorns. Moss clings to corners, and a low fog swirls just above the flagged floor, which is mostly covered in rush mats and strewn with fresh herbs.

The hall is filled with revelers feasting, toasting, and dancing, and I see immediately that they are not mortal, that they are impossible, that they are figures from children's stories and art prints purchased at renaissance festivals. They are at turns horned, winged, hoofed—some have hair the color of jewels and flowers—some have extra joints, others have too-long limbs—some have eyes that are too large and teeth that are too sharp. Some look *almost* mortal, like Morven and Maynard and Idalia, but they are so beautiful that a feeling of inhumanity lingers about them nonetheless.

And at any rate, this is no human banquet, at least not one I've ever seen or studied the likes of, because there is a real, honest-to-god *orgy* happening in front of the queen.

My pulse kicks up as we approach, and I get a good look at the array before us. Seven or eight fairies are knotted into a skein of spread limbs and arched necks, and the music of their fucking rivals the eerie music of the musicians. One fairy's wings shiver in pleasure as she sits atop another fairy's face. Something shimmering falls from her wings as she does, dusting her partner and the people fucking behind her too.

I shiver along with those wings. I want to be her, with her, under her. I want to see if an insatiable girl could get enough on that platform with them all.

The queen for her part seems unmoved by the display of hedonism in front of her or by any of the ancillary displays happening at the long tables and in the fog-bathed corners of the room. Her posture is gracefully erect, and her hands rest without either stiffness or restlessness on the arms of her throne, but she's as still as the rest of the room is not, and her gaze is remote and cool, as if her mind is on other things. I don't see how it could be—I've only been in this hall for ten seconds, and already I want to plonk down and watch everyone cavort and play for the next hundred years—but perhaps she's used to it. Or perhaps she expects it. It is her court to hold after all.

Bright but haunting music plays from a corner—played by

instruments I've seen more often in manuscripts than I have in real life: lutes and crumhorns and tabors.

I never imagined I would see them in real life next to a flipping *fairy orgy*, but there you are.

"Tonight begins the feast of Samhain," Felipe says in a low voice as he escorts me deeper into the hall. We pass a table with a horned fairy bent over its surface, his partner's hand on the back of his head to hold him down. His horns scratch the glossy wood as he's rutted into from behind, but when he catches me looking at him with concern, he gives me a feral smile. My heart kicks up another beat.

"Magic is stronger at Samhain," Felipe continues as we keep walking toward the throne. "And so are they. More dangerous too. More"—he seems to search for the right word —"*avid*. Take care."

Avid.

I glance around at the drinking and eating and dancing and fucking. Especially the fucking. It's as present as the smell of delicious food, as persistent as the music filling the hall.

I don't think I'll mind *avid* so much. It seems a lot like *insatiable*, and hell, if I have to be an abductee in fairyland, maybe I'll at least get to indulge myself a little. Or a lot.

My eyes slide back to the platform and then to the horned fairy being taken from behind.

Yes, *a lot* sounds very good at the moment.

"And I forgot to mention," Felipe says, and his voice is quicker now, more urgent, "that the fairy fruit that's written of in our world—"

"Yes, yes, I know," I say. "Don't eat the fruit."

Although when I glance around the hall again, it's hard to see what fruit the stories are talking about. There are piles of apples, bright red and shiny, and heaps of sloe berries, black-berries, raspberries, and plums. There are currants and hazel-nuts and roasted chestnuts, and wines and meads in clear pitchers, all in familiar shades of red and pink and pale gold. It all looks delicious, fruits and fruit drinks perfect for a harvest festival, but none of it looks remotely magical. Definitely not like the fairy-MDMA the stories make fairy fruit out to be.

"If only it were that simple," Felipe says, his voice getting even lower as we skirt the platform currently occupied with a fairy sex fest. But he sounds no less urgent. "The fairy fruit is not..."

But he stops, and when I glance over at him, I find the ancient Spaniard is *blushing*.

"Salt," he manages after a moment. "Mortal salt will fix almost anything."

I sense that he wants to say more but can't or won't find the words, and it doesn't matter now, because we're almost to the edge of the sex platform and to the dais where the queen sits.

Her throne is made of the same dark wood as the walls of the hall and is carved into the likeness of two stags standing amidst waving ferns, their proud wooden heads studded with real antlers, which twist and stretch into a web of bone above the queen's head. The queen's crown too is made of antlers, although they are far slenderer than the ones mounted on the throne. They twist once above her brow, and there are only a few thin branches spraying off from the main circle of the crown. I notice the tines are sharp enough to promise blood.

"Your Majesty," Felipe says as we finally clear the orgy and come to the foot of the throne. Letting go of my hand, he sinks to one knee with his hand over his heart, just as Maynard and the others did earlier in the library. A second too late, I follow, not nearly as practiced, but the long gown I'm wearing hiding the worst of it, I think.

"I hope you are having a good Samhain," the Spaniard continues. Out of the corner of my eye, I see his gaze is cast politely to the ground. "I found your guest and have brought her to you."

"My many thanks," the queen says in Latin. "And you may rise."

I'm not sure if I'm supposed to keep my eyes on the ground even after coming to my feet, but American that I am, my instinct is to make eye contact. Although when I do, I wish I were kneeling again.

The queen's eyes, although still cool as ever, are like the dark water under a new moon, promising eternity, promising endless, endless forever. And when they meet mine, I suddenly feel like that eternity already knows me, already sees me—sees too much of me.

I think it's fear that doses my blood then, but there are so many things like fear that speed the heart, and I don't want her to see that I'm breathing faster, shallower. Not if I'm supposed to take care, stay clever. To hide, I drop my gaze to her dramatic mouth and then to the rest of her. She's wearing a different dress now, a long-sleeved gown made of a black silk the same endless color as her eyes, its bodice dropping in a sharp V to just above her navel. I can see the contour of her clavicle, the inner curves of her breasts before they disappear behind the raw silk edge of the bodice. I can see the faint undulation of her breastbone, only visible as a suggestion in the fickle light of the chandeliers.

Aside from a gold signet ring on her smallest finger, she is otherwise free of jewels and gems, which seems strange for a queen, but I also can't imagine a necklace more finely wrought than the delicate berm of her collarbone, a pendant more exquisitely shaped than the stretch of her exposed sternum.

"Janneth," the queen says. "Sit next to me, please. Felipe, you may leave us."

I look over at Felipe, who gives me a look that suddenly reminds me very much of how Dr. Siska looks at students who plan on closing down a pub for a night. Like he's trying to beam the words *please be careful* right into my mind.

I can't imagine he ended up trapped here at the Stag Court for four hundred years because he was careful.

Still, I'm a little—okay, a lot—unnerved when he bows and takes his leave and I'm up on the dais alone with the queen. She indicates the undecorated chair next to her, which is made of the same wood as hers but carved only with the antler motifs, not in the likeness of the stags themselves. I sit, my heart pounding, trying to remember everything Felipe told me.

Fairies can't lie. Mortals need to eat salt. Bargain for my safety for the duration of my stay...I suppose with the queen, but as I steal a glance over at her, I have no idea what I could possibly offer her that she doesn't already have. She's a queen of a magic and seemingly immortal realm, with an entire court of orgy enthusiasts. Unless she needs a horny archaeologist at her disposal, I'm useless.

"So, Janneth Carter," the queen says in English, not looking at me. Her gaze is on the court, and from this angle, I can see the minute flicker of her stare. Far from being uninterested, she's absorbing everything, marking every laugh and moan. "I see you have met Felipe. I presume you no longer believe this to be a dream?"

"It seems safer to act as if everything is real and that everything matters. But I still find it all hard to believe," I answer honestly.

The queen keeps her eyes on the courtiers in front of us, but I see the small lift of her eyebrow. "You, who sift through mud and rocks hoping to find treasure, find this hard to believe? I should think you would be constructed entirely of belief, given your vocation."

I used to be, and I almost tell her that. I almost tell her that there used to be a Janneth who believed in everything. But I can't find the words.

It's bad enough to be insatiable, but to have been naive too? Gullible? I wouldn't want to admit that eagerness to anyone, much less a person as coldly regal as the queen.

"What do you want with me?" I ask instead. It might not be polite to do so, and it's certainly not strategic, but if I'm going to make it back home after my kidnapping sentence is over, I should probably get a sense of why I was taken in the first place.

My abruptness doesn't seem to bother the queen. Her tone of voice is the same as it was before when she says, "What do you think we want with you?"

"Morven said—" Even though I'm looking at countless people fucking in front of me right now, the words are still strange to say. "I'm to be a toy. That mortal toys are more fun."

The strange feeling is shame, I realize, but not humiliation at the prospect of being a toy. No, it's shame at how much the idea quickens heat inside me. Even the word *toy* has my thighs pressing together under the star-stitched skirt of my gown.

"Morven said that, did he?" the queen says, not seeming to expect an answer. "Interesting."

"It isn't true, then?" I ask. I can't tell if I sound hopeful or disappointed.

"Nothing is true until it is," the queen responds. The fairies really don't like giving straight answers. "But there is a tradition in Faerie, of mortals being taken at times when the veil is thin. Many are taken to be consorts to a lord or lady of Faerie. For a time."

"Is that why I was taken?"

The queen turns to look at me, her long, thick hair sliding over her shoulder as she does. She doesn't speak, but her eyes burn their way up my body, seeking out the corset-plumped curves of my breasts and the exposed flesh of my throat.

They stay the longest on my lips, and the longer she stares at my mouth, the hotter and hotter I feel, like a fever is burning inside me.

"Your Majesty," someone says from the floor below the dais, tearing us away from the moment. The queen and I both turn to look, and even though I shouldn't be surprised by anything anymore, I am shocked at the sight of him. He is impossibly slender, with pink-purple hair and green skin. He wears a collar of spiked leaves over a gold velvet jacket and hose.

When he sees he has our attention, he gives a bow.

"You flatter this servant to grace him with your attention. I come bearing a gift from the Queen of the Thistle Court, and I would have your permission to give it to you as a symbol of her friendship."

"Is that so?" the queen asks. Her hair shimmers as she leans forward on the throne. "Let's see it, then."

With a smile sharper than the leaves of his collar, the man from the Thistle Court pulls a small, silk-covered bundle from his pocket. He unwraps the bundle to reveal a delicate bracelet made of silver-set gems. They wink pink and purple and green in the light of the hall.

"My lady gives this to you as a token of her feelings," the servant says, stepping forward and giving another bow. He holds out both hands, the bracelet cradled in the silk it came in. "It is yours."

"The Court of Stags and the Court of Thistles used to be united, did they not?" the queen says. She doesn't move to take the bracelet, but she's still leaning forward, as if very interested in the servant and his gift.

"Yes, Your Majesty. A very long time ago, I believe."

"More than centuries," says the queen. "More than ages, if

the stories are to be believed. My great-grandmother had not yet been born, and the mortals outside our veil had not yet had their Christ."

The servant, while perhaps not expecting this digression, pivots smoothly. "And yet the Thistle Court will always and with great feeling remember the time our courts were as one."

"Oh," says the queen mildly, "I believe it. Put on the bracelet, please. I should like to see my gift on display."

For the first time, I see uncertainty hiccup through the servant. "Your Majesty, it would not be becoming for a lowly one such as myself to think of wearing such a—"

"Put on the bracelet," says the queen again, her voice still mild. But from nowhere, I see several fairies in russet-and-gold livery step forward. They have swords at their hips and pikes in their hands. The pikes are currently pointed straight at the ceiling, but the message is clear. The queen is not making a request.

The man from the Thistle Court swallows a final time. "Your Majesty," he whispers, but he seems to know his protests will get him nowhere but poked full of pike holes.

For my part, I'm not sure why he's so hesitant. Maybe it's some baroque court etiquette thing to not wear someone else's gift? But it's a simple enough choice: put on some jewelry, or get run through by a bunch of guards with very mean faces. Not that I understand why the queen is threatening him with pikes at all.

I shift uneasily on my seat, remembering once again Felipe's warnings about bargaining for safety.

With a shaking hand, the servant lifts the bracelet out of the silk and drapes it over his wrist. He's trembling so hard that the bracelet shivers over his skin, and then when he finally clasps the bracelet shut, he stumbles to the ground. At first I think it's because he's lost his balance or that he's perhaps thrown himself to the ground as a plea for mercy, but then a low tearing noise claws its way out of his throat, and I see he's gone taut with some kind of wordless agony.

The noise turns into a scream as thorns slowly push through his flesh, not big curved ones that grow on the stems of roses but thin ones growing as close together as barbs on a feather. Green liquid runs in narrow rivulets down his face, stains the white shirt pulled through the slashed silk of his jacket sleeves, drips off the long leaves of his collar.

It's his blood, I realize, far too late. He's bleeding all over from thousands of these thorn wounds, and it's because of—

The bracelet. The bracelet somehow did this.

I stand to—well, I don't know what I'm going to do—but a guard steps in front of me and gives me a forbidding look. I am not allowed to help. To interfere.

Shocked, I turn to stare at the queen. For her part, she seems completely unmoved, her expression unchanged by the man writhing in unimaginable pain before her feet. She watches him scream and bleed with almost nothing on her face, nothing at all, and there's no compassion at all in the slow, deliberate way she raises her hand.

One of her court guards goes to the servant and removes the bracelet from the servant. The thorns retreat, leaving so, so much viridian blood behind. It pools beneath him.

"Take the bracelet away from here," says the queen, voice as even as ever. "And take *him* to the dungeons."

The guards obey, expressions neutral as they heave the now-whimpering man from the floor and grab him by the wrists and ankles. The bracelet is carefully collected and carried behind the man it nearly killed. His blood is left there, shining slick and green.

The court—which had paused to watch the show—now returns to feasting with gusto, the music striking up even louder, the dancers laughing, the lovers moaning. It's not as if it hasn't happened. It's as if it happening energized them. It's as if it happening was exciting and good.

And that's when the fear comes back, a wave of it so heavy that I think I might drown. I sit, stunned and sick.

"You knew something was wrong with it," I say numbly to the queen, who's now settled back on the throne. A small smile haunts her lips—the first smile I've seen from her.

It's beautiful. And terrifying.

"Of course, I knew," replies the queen, looking out at her reveling court, reveling all the harder with blood spilled on the floor. Some even come forward and drag their fingertips through it before sucking their hands clean with relish or offering their fingers to lovers to lick clean. Green smears their mouths and drips down their chins.

The fear is a thousand tiny bugs crawling on the inside of my skin now.

"But how? He said—" I think back to the servant's words, trying to filter through exactly what he said and how he phrased it. "He spoke of friendship. And Felipe told me fairies can't lie."

"The *friendship* between my court and the Court of Thistles is one marked by cairns and crow-circled battlefields. A token of their lady's feelings would only be something meant to make me suffer. You look surprised, Janneth, but I suppose it's good that you see this now: there are more ways to lie than just with words."

I can't believe she's talking to me so calmly, so levelly, after watching that fairy screaming and punctured on the floor. I can't believe I'm talking back to her.

And that's not the worst of it, actually. The worst is that I'm not sure how I feel about watching that fairy bleed, because if the queen had not asked him to put on that bracelet —if she had not seen through the trick—then it would have been her bleeding. Her screaming.

And I do not like that thought either.

I like it even less.

"I'm sorry," I say, still numb. "I'm sorry they tried to hurt you."

"Do not be," says the queen dismissively. "I'm yet unafraid of the Thistle Court and its lady. Although I am insulted that she thought I wouldn't see through that little trick of hers. But perhaps returning the bracelet to her with her servant's severed hand inside it will remind her to try harder to kill me."

The remark about the servant's severed hand is so casually, effortlessly *cruel* that I have a moment where I don't fully understand it, where I think I must have misheard.

But I know I didn't.

And I know I'm not imagining that the queen is in a slightly better mood now. Her mouth is softer, as if her smile might return, and I see her long fingers move in time with the music. She's happy. There's blood on the floor and on the mouths of her people, and she's happy.

I take a deep breath and look down at my own hands. They are attached to my body, and they aren't covered in thorns or blood. For now. It's becoming very clear to me that I don't have any way to predict the caprice and cruelty of this place. Of the fairies here. Of *her*. It could be me screaming on the floor next, and as I look around the room at the banquet, I feel the creeping sense that any one of these people could be the ones to do it, to make me scream. Even if they didn't hurt me, they would watch. They would do nothing to help.

You should not feel safe. Message received, Felipe. Loud and clear.

The folk here love a bargain above all else; they love price.

You might be able to buy some safety that way.

I see the necessity of it even more now. If a bargain is what it takes to keep me safe until I figure out how to escape or

Samhain ends and I'm sent back home, then a bargain is what I shall strike.

Although, fuck me, what can I offer? Sex? I'm not averse in the least to bargaining with sex—I like to have it, and being in the queen's bed sounds *amazing*. But the orgy platform in front of me is full of fairies flexible enough to put circus performers to shame, and sex is free for the taking everywhere else in the room. I can't see how sex with me would be a very tempting offer. Like offering a nickel to a billionaire.

Think, Janneth. Think.

I could talk to her about excavation strategies, I guess. Demonstrate how to make tea on a dig site with nothing but a camping stove and a willingness to get burned. What a fairy queen would want with that information, I don't know, but it's all I've got. I don't know how to fight or enchant bracelets; I don't know how to do anything other than like history and sex and crave more from life than life can possibly give me. I'm just a mortal girl in fairyland, with nothing but myself to offer.

But maybe that's it? Morven had said mortal toys were more fun, after all, and the way the queen had looked at me when we were talking of consorts...

Well, I will never know if I don't try, and if I don't try, I might end up bleeding on the floor. So.

"Your Majesty," I say, knowing I sound a little clumsy saying the courtly words but forging ahead anyway, "I want to make a bargain with you."

This catches her attention, because for the first time at the banquet, she truly looks at me. "A bargain, Janneth Carter?"

Her voice is soft, dangerous even, but I continue, "Surely better than a stolen mortal consort is a mortal happy to be one. Guarantee me that you will add my safety to the promise you made in the library, and in return, I'll promise my willingness to you. To be your companion, your consort. To be whatever you wish until Samhain is over."

"Even if what I wish for is not a companion or consort?" Her voice is silky. "Even if I wish for a toy or a pet instead?"

I have the sudden image of being curled naked at her feet, her long fingers stroking my hair. I swallow.

"Then I will be your pet."

"And remind me of this promise I made in the library?"

"That I will stay here for two nights, and then on the third, you'll let me leave Faerie. All I'm asking for is that you promise my safety too."

The queen gives me an appraising look, as if sifting through my words. Then she turns and gestures at her court, at the sex and excess, at the glinting jewels and sweat-shimmered skin. "And what, Janneth Carter, can you give me that I do not already have at a wave of my hand? You say you will offer me your willingness, but that is not in short supply here. Do you think the people at my court would be unwilling to come to my bed?"

"No, Your Majesty."

"So again, I ask: What can you truly offer me for this additional promise?"

I know that it's important that I do not lie, so I can't make up an answer for her. I can't invent something out of thin air. It needs to be the truth, but now I'm right back where I started, because the truth is that I have nothing at all to offer a queen like this one—

My eyes land on the orgy in front of me, on the twisting, moving bodies. But now I'm looking past the moving hands and hips, past the spread thighs and braced knees. I see the fairies' faces: their glazed eyes, their bored expressions. And with that in mind, the slow caresses and even slower kisses take on a new meaning. Not *savoring* slow but *desultory* slow. Not lingering but uninterested.

Maybe an immortal lifetime filled with every kind of pleasure does that to someone; maybe it's possibly to eventually become blasé about what some people crave beyond all reason.

But I think I'm personally a very, very long way from that *maybe*. So long that it might take an eternity for me to be sated.

"I will always want more," I say, turning back to look at her. "That's what I can offer. I will always, *always* want more."

Her attention is wholly on me now. "Oh?"

She doesn't believe me, I think. There's a slight arch to her brow, a skeptical tilt of her head. I imagine she's seen enough people grow bored with indulgence to think I'm spinning tales, childishly asserting things I cannot possibly know about what *always* will mean to me.

And in one way, she might be right to doubt, because I can't know what *always* will mean to me. But I do know *me* —I know who Janneth Carter, horny archaeologist, is.

And if there was ever a time for insatiability to be a super-power, then this is it.

I stand and meet the queen's stare, pretending I know exactly what the fuck I'm doing.

"I'll prove it," I say lightly and step off the dais.

CHAPTER 7

"Janneth," the queen calls.

I'm off the dais now, and so I have to look up at her on her throne. The antlers twisting from the back of the throne stretch behind her, and from this angle, they look like they're part of her crown and maybe like they're a part of her. It's unnerving.

It's beautiful too.

She doesn't speak for a moment, and I barely know this woman or this place, and so I have no idea if she'll speak to forbid me from doing something stupid or if she'll goad me into doing something even stupider.

But when she speaks, it's neither warning nor encouragement. "Your dress," she says.

I look down and see the edge of my hem has dragged against the small lake of green blood on the floor. It's grown even darker since it first spilled, nearly black at its perimeter, and now the blush-colored fabric of my dress is stained with it.

I have a moment of—well, *blankness* is the wrong word. But so is *horror*.

It is the space where horror should go, I think, where

disgust and terror should twist together, but instead there is nothing, an emptiness. Just the feeling that I should be more upset than I am. That I should not already be turning around and continuing to the platform.

That I should not already be thinking of mouths and hands and spread thighs...

But here I am at the edge of the platform, my dress wet with blood, my heart thumping against my chest not with fear but with lust. Or perhaps the fear is still there, but it's feeding the lust too, because there is something thrilling, however sick, in feeling afraid and aroused at the same time.

I'm about to crawl right into the fray—the few sex parties I've been to have taught me the valuable lesson that there's a time and a place for shyness, and orgies are not it—when I feel a finger run over my shoulder. A moth flits above the moaning pile atop the platform.

I turn to see Idalia, dressed in silver, her moths no longer around her neck but high above her pewter head like a cloud. And then behind me, I feel another presence. Maynard.

"Pretty things should be played with," Idalia murmurs, coming closer. She leans down to speak in my ear, her lips warm against my skin. "Is that what you want?"

"Yes," I murmur back. I mean, I wasn't about to climb into an orgy to ask about skin-care routines.

"Both of us will play with you, if you'll have us," Idalia purrs, a hand trailing down my back to find the laces of the dress's corset. "Right here, in front of the queen."

"Do I—is there—" I've never needed to have this conversation with people who weren't human before. And I'm not worried about contraception—I just had my shot last week, but there are other things to worry about it. "When fairies and humans are together...I mean, to be safe—"

Idalia nips at the lobe of my ear. "Fairies and humans can't pass infections to each other, if that's what you're wondering.

But you might have to think about what else you'd like *safe* to mean. For example, does *safe* mean no pain?" She sinks her teeth into the place between my neck and my shoulder now. I shudder, the pain streaking through my body like rain, washing me clean. Leaving me hot and shivery.

"Or does *safe* mean no shame?" Maynard says in my other ear, his rich voice turning the last word into a melody of lust. His hand has joined Idalia's on the back of my dress, and the laces are being loosened, loosened, until I feel the front of the dress start to gape and sag in front.

"I like both of those things," I say, a little breathlessly.

"You need only cry mercy," Maynard says, "and we will give it. But mortals so rarely ask for mercy, do they? Especially if they've already tasted what we can offer..."

Tasted.

I wonder if he means the fairy fruit. Thank god I'm not foolish enough to eat any while I'm here.

Maynard's words have distracted me from the work of his fingers, and I'm surprised at the brush of cool air on my breasts as the bodice slips down to my waist. Idalia is kissing my neck now, and I'm being guided to sit on the edge of the platform, and then Maynard is kissing my neck too, while the fairies behind us move to greet me, more kisses trailing along the bare skin between my shoulder blades, hands languorous on my hips.

Idalia's fingers find my nipples—erect and sensitive—and roll them cleverly between her fingertips. Heat sparks at her touch, those sparks tracing down like falling fireworks to my cunt, and it's only then that I lift my head to see if the queen is watching.

She is.

She is watching.

She seems as remote as ever on her throne—there's still no reading those black eyes or that elegant mouth—but there is something alert in her posture that wasn't there before. As if her motionlessness now is intentional rather than habitual.

Her eyes are on mine as Maynard and Idalia together ruck up my skirt. I'm grateful that I'm wearing my usual black boy shorts today—comfortable but cute—and that I chose this dress, which pools around my waist in pretty, filmy layers as the two fairies push my skirt higher and higher. Some people have princess fantasies—I have fantasies about getting railed in a princess dress. To each their own, I guess.

"What a picture," Maynard says, stroking over the colorful tattoo on my thigh. I look down to see his fingertip skate over the inked folds of the Belle Dame's red dress. "And here you've been pretending to be ignorant of all to do with our kind."

"The tales she hears are hardly real knowledge, Maynard," Idalia says. Her fingers join his over the tattoo. "Whatever germs of truth may lie dormant inside them."

"I got it years ago," I say, although I'm not sure why it matters. Nothing matters except the long-fingered caresses on my thigh, nothing matters except the queen watching me from her throne.

"I'm curious," Maynard says, "when you look at this picture, who do you wish to be? The merciless woman, vain and beautiful? Or her bewitched lover, doomed as he may be?"

I am sitting with my breasts bared and my skirt up to my waist, and still I flush. I fear the answer will reveal more about myself than I'd like.

"No need to answer," Idalia says, a smile curling her silver-painted lips. "The queen already knows."

"But there is plenty she does not know yet," Maynard says, and then he pushes my thighs apart.

Someone's touch skates over the soft fabric of my under-wear, light as a feather, and I catch my breath. I want to rock my hips into the sensation, but the fairies behind me hold my hips in place as they kiss my back and neck.

My hair is swept out of the way so they can kiss more of me; Maynard teases a stiff nipple where it juts through the hair tossed over my shoulder.

"What lovely little shivers you make," Idalia says. "And we haven't even gotten to my favorite part."

"What's your—" But I don't need to finish the question. She and Maynard are already tugging my panties down. It's over before I can worry about how awkward it is, how inelegant. How the queen probably doesn't have to wriggle out of a cotton-Lycra blend in order to be touched.

"This," Idalia says as I'm bared completely to view and Maynard's large hands keep my thighs prised apart. "This is my favorite part."

No one is touching my cunt, but I'm already quivering like they are, I'm already trying to arch and seek. The hands on my hips won't let me, though, and the more I try to squirm, the more Maynard pulls his hands away from my breasts.

"No, no," he scolds. "This isn't for you."

I'm being stripped down and held open, kissed along my back and neck and shoulders—how can it not be *for me*?

But then I look up again and see the queen on her throne, her eyes dark and inscrutable, and I realize Maynard is right. This isn't for me.

I marched over to prove something to her, to show her I knew better than she did, but I feel like I'm the one being shown instead.

Not that it makes any material difference: her doing this to me, having her courtiers spread me like a butterfly and expose me to her gaze, makes it even hotter.

Maynard is the first to touch my pussy, and the difference between *careful* and *teasing* is evident in the wickedness of his expression as he sands his fingertips over my curls. I try to arch again, but it's futile. I am held in place, forced to endure the torture of his slow exploration.

Idalia bends her head and pulls the furled tip of my breast between her lips. The shock of her hot, wet mouth around such a sensitive part of me makes me gasp. Maynard responds by running a finger up the center of me—and I knew I was aroused, but even *I'm* surprised to feel how wet I am when he touches me.

Up on the dais, the queen doesn't move, doesn't seem to react at all, but neither can I tear my gaze away from hers as Maynard finds the swollen part of me and teases it with his middle finger. As I writhe against the many hands holding me in place, I am also held fast by the queen's attention, by the way she watches me like I'm the only person in the teeming hall.

It's only when her stare drops from my face down to my breasts and then to my cunt that I feel released from her hold, but I still don't feel entirely free of her. In fact, maybe I'm more in her thrall than before, watching her as she watches me, as she observes Maynard and Idalia expertly coaxing me into breathless pleasure.

It's been months since I've been fucked by someone— even longer since I've been *properly* fucked—and it's an embarrassingly short journey from my panties coming off to everything pulling tight and hot below my navel, a shimmering knot tied around my clit that is ready to unravel at the slightest touch.

The fairies behind us—the ones kissing and nuzzling me —slide their hands past my hips to my thighs, which they now hold open for Maynard and the queen. And with me pinned and peeled like fruit, Maynard finally rubs my clit the way I need, with hard circles and presses. Between his touch and Idalia's wicked mouth toying with my nipple, I'm done for, but with the queen watching, I'm *extra* gone. I want her to see me come. I want her to make me come. I want her to heap more of everything on top me—pain, humiliation, sheer obscenity—and I want her to see how I can take it, how I was born to drink it all down, swallow every last drop.

"Isn't she pretty?" Idalia says, pulling back to brush my hair from my flushed face. Her own face is hauntingly beautiful in the mingled gold and silver glow of the chandeliers and mycelium threads. High, rounded cheekbones, a full mouth in the shape of a heart and painted bright silver. Long lashes and eyes a deep, deep brown. Her pewter dress is thin enough that I can see the press of her own nipples against the fabric.

"She is," Maynard agrees. His hand has gentled between my legs now, but it doesn't feel like it's out of kindness or care for how sensitive I am after coming. It's so he can study me, so he can observe which caresses make me strain against the hands holding me in place and which give me time to breathe and compose myself.

Then he looks back to the queen, who lifts her fingers from the arm of her throne. I don't know what the gesture means until I do: Idalia's hand joins Maynard's, and I feel the warm slide of her fingers inside me at the same time as Maynard starts thumbing my clit without mercy.

I peak even faster this time, my body trying so hard to curl around itself, a cry spilling from my lips as my pussy squeezes around Idalia's fingers and my heart hammers against my chest. The orgasm abates, but as usual, it leaves hunger in its wake. Hunger for more, always more. The kind of more that tires out lovers and kinksters and entire rooms of partners.

Except *tire* seems to be the last verb I'd use in this room—far from it. My little demonstration seems to have energized the banquet; the music is louder, the fucking at the tables more vigorous. Even the languid orgy behind me has changed: I can feel the pants and rocks of the fairies holding my thighs and kissing my back as they're fucked from behind, feel the eager way they fondle and lick at me.

The queen lifts her fingers again, and this time, Maynard moves off the platform to kneel in front of me. His mouth is at the level of my sex. A thick erection presses against his breeches.

Idalia reaches down and spreads my intimate flesh as much as it can be spread, until I know my erect clit and glistening entrance must be painfully available for viewing. The sheer lewdness of it is arousing, the shame of it like a drug I've been searching for my entire life.

The queen is still sitting as regally as ever, but I see the rise and fall of her chest, even from the platform some ways away from the throne. She's breathing harder. And her hand—where it rests on the arm of the throne, it's now curling into a tight fist.

Maynard leans in and gives me a long, savoring lick, slick and ticklish, and then wastes no time getting to business. He dips his face low and starts feasting on my pussy, with laves and circles that have my toes curling in my slippers. Pleasure twines through my belly once more, stoked by shame and the wonderful, horrible feeling of being spread and on display, and it's too much to take in, not only the fucking around me and right behind me, but Maynard's head moving between my legs, the sight of all those hands on my thighs, the blood-stained skirt of my fairy-tale dress shoved up to my waist to make room for it all.

Idalia takes hold of my jaw with the hand that was inside me just a moment ago and forces me to look straight ahead.

At the queen.

"Eyes up, Janneth," Idalia purrs. "Eyes on your queen."

My queen.

It doesn't sound wrong at all, and that's what I'd essentially promised, right? To be the queen's in exchange for her keeping me safe until my release? And once again, I think about how it's not that bad a deal when it's all said and done... I mean, I would rather have not been kidnapped at all, but all things considered, there are worse fates than being a fairy queen's sex pet.

The queen's stare trails up from where Maynard's head moves between my legs up to my face, and then our eyes meet and lock. Her eyes are as wet and black as the sea at night as she watches me, and when the next climax rolls through my body, brought on by Maynard's clever mouth and her cool appraisal, I feel something almost like awe, like reverence.

Like relief.

The rolling waves of pleasure push their way out from my center to the soles of my feet and the tips of my fingers, and I am past soft cries and bitten-off moans now, I am whimpering, I am keening, I am making noises that should embarrass me— that *do* embarrass me but that also feed the sweet, hungry shame that makes all of this so much closer to my fantasies than anything I've found in the real world.

The climax recedes, and though I know I could happily take more (and more still), I'm also shivering and spent in the arms of the fairies holding me.

For the first time since I entered the hall, the queen stands. She descends the dais with eerie grace and strides to the platform, where I am half-undressed, wet, and restrained not by cuffs or bonds but by hands. Hands that sometimes have too many knuckles or claws instead of nails. Hands that seem to have acted with her will and at her behest.

The queen stops just in front of me, the silk of her gown swishing against the rush mats on the floor. Though she seems as remote as ever, up close I see the thrum of her pulse in her neck. The rose bloom of color on her cheeks.

She lowers a hand and then runs her fingers through the

wet mess of my cunt. Her touch is curious but also laden with prerogative. I'm hers to touch as she pleases now.

I start panting, as much at that thought as at the actual touch.

Without a word, she presses her fingers—slick with me—to my lips, and when I open for her, she pushes her fingers into my mouth.

I suck, obediently, instinctively, and though it's a tiny, tiny thing, I see her swallow.

"Fine, then, Janneth Carter," she says, pulling her fingers free and leaving my mouth too cold and too empty. "You have my agreement. You shall be my pet, my everything, until the final night of Samhain, and you will not be harmed until you leave Faerie."

She steps back, and to the rest of the hall, she says, "This is my consort, a mortal worthy of a stag's heart and a stag's kiss. So too shall she be worthy of a stag's fate. Feast her well."

Cheers resound around the room, as if I'm being welcomed into a sexy but proud family, and she touches my face with wet fingers.

"You've done well," she says softly. "And I greatly look forward to seeing you on the morrow for the hunt."

And then she sweeps away with her guards and leaves the fairies to their dark, dangerous revels without her supervision.

CHAPTER 8

I am given cool rags to clean up with, and then I'm perched at the head of a long table and fed extravagant foods—venison pies topped with elaborate shiny crusts, seared larks, and roasted swans with outstretched wings and eyes made of sloe. Hippocras jellies and rosewater tarts, wines and meads and confections of spun sugar so delicate they melt on my tongue. The raw fruit I forbear to eat for now, until I can make sure I'm not going to enchant myself with an apple slice or something, and I sprinkle a little mortal salt on everything I eat, even on the sweet things and in the wine.

Felipe was right earlier, and at every table, I see vessels for holding salt—ornate containers made of gold and glass and gems, in the shapes of great ships and singing mermaids. I also see I'm not the only one making use of them, although out of the entire hall, there are only two or three of us. But still, I draw some comfort from the fact I'm not the only mortal here. Not counting Felipe, who seems to be in a four-hundred-year-old category of his own.

I ask the fairies eating with me about the hunt tomorrow, and I'm told it will not matter that I've never hunted before and I'm not exactly an equestrian. *It's primarily the queen's hunt, really,* they explain. *A private Samhain tradition.*

I'm not the one being hunted, am I? I ask them, entirely serious, and they laugh and laugh like I've told the world's funniest joke.

What a waste of you that would be!

Which isn't exactly reassuring, but I still extract from one of them that I'll be unhunted tomorrow, which allows me some measure of relief.

The revel seems unending. The fucking goes on and so does the dancing and feasting, and at some point, I find my eyes sliding closed and my head slumping against Idalia's shoulder.

"Go to bed, little mortal," she chides.

"I don't know if I can find my way back to my room," I admit. Felipe is no longer in the hall, and I'd feel like a child asking Idalia or Maynard for help finding my way back.

"The leaves are waiting outside the door for you, are they not?" Idalia says, the same way someone might explain how sidewalks work. The moth bobbing next to her face seems equally bewildered by my ignorance, because it flaps in place for a long minute, antennae moving in my direction, before finally drifting toward the more educated banquet guests.

I grab my coat from the dais and stumble, tipsy and full, to the doors of the hall and open them to find the orange and ruby leaves waiting for me. I follow them through even more unfamiliar spaces—galleries and grand staircases I'm certain I haven't seen before—and then past a shadowed opening that looks like it leads to some sort of large chamber.

"Have fun?" a voice calls from the darkness.

I stop—the leaves sighing as they too stop and sift backward in my direction—and I peer into the murk. A few solitary candles flicker at the front of the space, illuminating pews and a carved rood screen. There are statues and painted panels and a gleaming font at the front. It is almost like a chapel, like a church, although I don't see anything recognizably Christian about it—or recognizably mortal, for that matter.

Morven steps forward, still wearing his outfit of all black, his cape swaying around him as he stops.

"I did," I say.

"It's good that you enjoyed yourself tonight," he says. The shadows seem to hang off his eyelashes and cling to the underside of his lush mouth. "It will not last long."

"Yeah, because I'm leaving as soon as I can," I say. The wine sharpens both my attraction and my irritation. "You can stop being so grumpy with me, by the way. I didn't ask to get kidnapped."

"And I didn't ask to kidnap you," Morven says. "But it is my sister who wears the crown, and so I'm hers to command until my oath of fealty has ended. However long that might take," he adds, and then he strides out of the chapel and into the daedal knot of the castle. Even his stride is brooding, unhappy.

I wonder if the queen knows how much her brother dislikes serving her. I wonder if treason is ever on his mind.

When I get to my room, the leaves sag to the floor in apparent relief, and I open the door to find a steaming bath waiting for me in the middle of the room. Rose petals—a red so dark they're nearly black—swirl on the surface of the water, and on a table next to the enormous copper tub are various soaps and oils as well as a large linen towel.

I strip, throw my bloodstained dress over a nearby chair, and climb naked into the bath before washing and soaking until I'm clean and limp-limbed. Between the feast and the orgasms and now the hot scented bath, I must admit Faerie has charms to counterbalance its bloody horrors.

Also its penchant for kidnapping.

After a long time soaking and staring at the moon outside

my window, I climb out of the bath and dry off. In the wardrobe, I find a long robe made of a soft ivory fabric, thin enough to show the shadow of my navel underneath, and I walk over to the bed. It's a four-poster, etched with roses and spiral motifs, the head of it carved with the same antler-headed man from the door of the room. The curtains are a plush green velvet, embroidered with raven-colored rose petals, and the sheets are a silk so white and crisp that they remind me of freshly fallen snow.

I don't lie down. I stand with one hand on the curtains, my fingers moving idly over the sable blooms—blooms that are so close to the color of the queen's eyes.

This is my consort, a mortal worthy of a stag's heart and a stag's kiss.

I don't know what I feel right now. The night went about as well as a night in fairyland could go—I'm not enchanted or dead, and I've struck a bargain that will help me get back, safely, to my own world. Plus I had great sex.

So why am I suddenly so restless that I can't stand it?

Is it greediness? Loneliness? Fear?

I walk to the door and open it, unsurprised to see the leaves shivering on the floor.

"I don't know where I want to go," I say, which is a lie and I'm not supposed to lie here...although maybe lying to the leaves doesn't count. They continue to tremble in place, but there's something judgmental about it now.

"Okay, fine," I concede. "I do know where I want to go. I want to go to her."

The leaves start moving, like they thought I'd never ask, and soon we're moving through the castle again. Again, it's almost all unfamiliar to me, and I know if I were to attempt an escape, my best shot would be while I was outside the castle walls. I don't know if I can even find my way to the front door on my own—and I feel like the enchanted leaves are probably not enchanted to help the queen's prisoners escape.

After a long climb, I find myself in another tower, standing in front of a door lacquered to a red gleam. I hesitate a moment, feeling stupid in my see-through robe and having no good reason to knock on her door.

But the leaves brush against the wood, as if saying, *Stop being such a coward, this is the right door*—and then the door swings open of its own volition, revealing a chamber much like my own, but much larger, and much more...well, much more *her*.

Rather than roses, the room is carved, stitched, and painted with stags and antler motifs, to the point where some of the stools and chairs have legs made of antler and bone. The tester of her canopy bed is likewise made of antlers, and the silk curtains hanging from them are the rust-red color of the hills in autumn.

A large desk is set below one of the windows, and shelves and shelves of books line most of the space—enough to make me wonder how there are still more to fill the library downstairs. Roses climb up the walls on the far side of the room, full-blown and weeping dark petals onto the floor, and near the desk I see the denuded stem of a single rose, its shredded petals withered on the loose papers scattered across the desk. Like someone had plucked the living rose from the wall for the sole purpose of tearing it apart.

It's the large copper tub in the center of the room that snares my attention in the end. A twin to the one in my room, it's also dotted with rose petals, and it makes me wonder if the petals in my own tub had come from here, from this room.

If maybe the queen herself had chosen the roses for my bath.

And even more than the tub itself, it's the woman sitting inside it that draws me to a halt. The only other person in this room. Her dark hair is piled atop her head and secured in place with two pins of bone. Damp tendrils curl at the nape of her neck, and water glistens along the elegant curve of her shoulders. And her back...

I draw closer without meaning to, not sure I'm seeing correctly at first. The light from the fire only does so much, and the single candle flickering on the table next to the copper tub creates tricks of shine and shadows.

But no, as I step forward, I see the light hasn't betrayed me: just below the wing of her scapula, her pale skin goes clear and translucent, like glass. And after a feathering of trapezius muscle, the muscle too turns clear, so I can see the articulation of her spine and the graceful arcs of her ribs. And past them, the red bellows of her lungs.

I can see *inside* her body.

I'm frozen, staring at her back, at this so very inhuman part of her, when she speaks without turning around.

"Come here, Janneth," says the queen, and I obey, hoping she's not absolutely furious with me for walking in on her naked and bathing.

"I'm sorry, Your Majesty," I say, sinking to a knee when I reach her, making sure to bow my head too. "The leaves opened the door, and I know I shouldn't have come inside, but I didn't notice you at first—"

"But you did notice me, and you still stayed," the queen observes mildly. "Well, if you're here, I may as well put you to use."

I think of the way she looked at my mouth in the hall, and I flush hot.

"Yes," I whisper, half eagerness, half fear. "I'll be of use."

"You may look up, Janneth," the queen says, sounding amused. "I'm not a Gorgon."

"Are Gorgons real too? Like fairies?" I ask, looking up to see we're nearly at eye level like this. Tiny water droplets hang in the hair that's come loose from the knot on her head and slide down her collarbone and chest, and I can't help but be aware of how naked she is below the petal-strewn water of the bath.

I want to look so badly, I want to touch, and perhaps she knows what I'm thinking, because she gives an imperial tilt of her head to the edge of the table, where a small cloth is folded next to the soap.

"Wash me," the queen orders, and I move to obey, rolling up the sleeves of my robe and settling myself behind her. My hand trembles a little as I dip the linen in the water and then ready it with soap. And it's ridiculous given the things I've gotten up to before now. Washing someone's back shouldn't rob me of breath.

But here I am, shaking and practically panting, while the air smells of soap and there's metal and gallons of water separating my body from hers.

I press the wet, soapy cloth to her back and drag it up, carrying warm water with it, and she lets out a sigh that's so human I nearly drop the cloth.

And then I find myself eager to hear it again. And again.

"Yes, Gorgons are real," she says after a minute. "As real as you or me. Most things are real, nightmares and dreams both. Sometimes," she says, a wet, slender hand toying with a floating petal, "the dreams become nightmares."

I'm watching the water sluice down her back, over a tableau of things never meant to be seen: muscles rippling, lungs swelling and shrinking, bones still pink with blood.

It should be horrific, it should be wrong, and yet it is so beautiful that I find myself speechless. Except to say: "Sometimes the opposite is true, Your Majesty."

She doesn't speak at that, and the only answer is the crackling of the fire and the drip of the water. The wind buffeting the castle from outside. And then she finally replies, "This is true."

I begin washing an arm, moving to the side so I can wash all the way down to her fingertips, and then I do the other side as well, wondering how *much* she'd like me to wash her, because the innocent places are dwindling.

She settles the question by settling back against the tub, arching her long neck as she rests her head against the edge and closes her eyes. "You may continue," she says, in a regal, used-to-being-obeyed manner. And so I do, soaping her neck and chest and breasts—high handfuls with tips that grow taut and stiff as I massage the cloth over them. The front of her is not translucent like her back, at least as far as I can see, but there is a faint flush on her chest from the warmth of the water. Maybe from something else.

I clean my way down her stomach, and then her thighs part under the water, as if in unconscious response.

"Have you ever been someone's pet before?" she asks. Her eyes are still closed.

I'm glad of it, because I don't want her to see whatever's on my face right now.

Lust, shame. Longing.

"Not for lack of trying," I say. I try to make it light, but it comes out the way it feels. Which is lonely.

"Humans don't often want to be pets," she remarks.

"I used to want nothing more," I say, breathing out as I feel the tight divot of her navel beneath my fingers. "But no one wanted me. So I told myself to stop wanting it altogether because it hurt less that way. Because then it felt like a choice."

I can't believe I just admitted that out loud. *Shit*. The last thing I want is for the queen to know what a needy, lonely mess I am.

"I find it hard to believe no one wanted you," the queen says.

I try to explain in a way that doesn't make me sound too pathetic. "Do you remember when I told you that I always want more?"

"Yes."

"It's not—an easy thing. For a lover. Even a"—I'm not sure if they know these words in Faerie, but I go on anyway—"even a Dominant has limits on how much they want to give. Even the people who say they want a twenty-four-seven submissive find themselves sick of me. Because I want to be pushed further and longer. Because I want more and more and more. It's greed. It's too much. I'm too much."

I break off, pissed at myself. I should not have said all that. I didn't even *want* to say all that, not out loud, not to her, and I'm hot with embarrassment. I don't want to be needy or grasping or pitiable. I've spent so much time trying to corral myself into a respectable archaeologist precisely so I *wouldn't* be those things.

But the queen seems unfazed by it. There is no distaste in her expression, no pity. Her eyes are open but hooded, and she stares at me.

"There is not so much difference between those with the greed to take and the greed to make," she murmurs. "Both are hard ways to be. Both are lonely."

I duck my head, unable to take her gaze right now. Not that looking at where I'm washing her stomach is helping my composure. Between the drifting petals, I see the delta of her sex: a delicate triangle of curls, a glimpse of dark pink under the ripples of the water.

"Janneth," says the queen. Her voice is quiet. "Take care of me as a pet should."

There can be no question of what she means, and I'm surprised at the relief I feel at the command. Like maybe part of me was worried I was too much to have even as a bargain consort-pet. Even for an immortal fairy who smiles when her enemies bleed at her feet.

I drop the cloth under the water and then splay my hand directly on the warm skin of the queen's stomach. I feel the muscles underneath, taut and still, and then she exhales as I push my hand lower.

Her curls are shockingly soft, and when I trail my fingers to where her body opens, I find her slick even in the water. Slick enough to make everything slippery. Slick enough that she must have been ready for this for quite some time.

She closes her eyes, a faint shiver going through her as I graze her clitoris, stiff and needy at the apex of her. "Yes," she says. Only that.

"You...you should tell me what you like," I say, sliding the pad of my finger over her swollen clit again.

The queen opens her eyes to blink at me, as if this is the most surprising thing I've done all night. Not march up to an orgy to prove a point, not come into her rooms at night unannounced. But the small, almost-pedestrian question about how she likes her cunt touched.

"It pleases me to have you as my pet," she says finally and then closes her eyes. "And so whatever you do, I shall find pleasing, because you are mine."

"Oh," I say, without meaning to have made a noise at all. But somehow she said the one thing I've been needing to hear for years.

I am pleasing. *I am hers.*

Even abducted, scared—even with a bloodstained dress still crumpled up in my room—the words thrill me.

I lower my head again so she can't see me swallow, fight back a giddy smile, blink back tears. I'm a fucking mess.

"And trust that I will not be shy about taking what I want regardless," she says, her tone casual and unbothered, like she hasn't just spoken aloud one of my most secret appetites, like she hasn't just given me a promise I wish for all the world she will keep.

Lust swims through my blood as I caress the tumid part of her that needs touching, slowly at first. Not because I particularly think she wants gentle but because I don't want it to feel like I'm trying to rush this.

I want her to know I love being her pet, for however short a time I'll be one. And that if there'd been no bargain at the banquet, no transaction of safety, I'd probably be here anyway, offering myself up for her to use however she'd like.

Her eyes are still closed, her red lips parted the smallest amount. Her stomach hitches when I change my strokes from up and down to side to side, her thighs falling as far apart as they can in the tub. The water sloshes; petals stick to my arm and to her breasts. There's a scent on the air that's so heady I can barely stand it, and it's not the petals in the bath or the roses blooming on the wall, and it's not the soap I used to wash the queen, and it's not anything I can even describe, because what it smells like makes no sense. It smells like the way I felt as a teenager at my first girlfriend's house, the blankets over our heads as we kissed for the very first time in the dark. It smells like Edinburgh at night when the fog is up and the lamps are lit against smoke-stained walls and every narrow alley beckons me forward to find its secrets.

It smells the way I used to feel about magic and history and secrets. Like something more was waiting for me—like if I just went to the right *place*, just turned the right page, just cracked open my chest a little bit more, I would find a special story meant only for me. A special destiny, a special life.

That's the smell in the air.

And also it makes me hungry. Ferociously hungry. My mouth is watering.

The queen takes my hand and, with imperial assurance, pushes my fingers down to the slick breach of her body. She barely waits for the two fingers I give her before she rocks her hips into my hand, fucking herself not only on my fingers but against the heel of my palm.

The balls of her feet are braced against the tub as she arches. She's so soft inside that I think I might die.

She climaxes abruptly, faster than I would've thought it would take, and there's a distant part of me that wonders if it's been a long time for her, like it had been for me. If even in a court of orgies and excess, she's denied herself to the point where a hand between her legs in the bath is such a relief that it only takes two minutes for her body to culminate.

She turns her head away as she comes, toward the far wall, so I can only see the long line of her neck, her hair sticking to it, and the curve of her cheek and jaw. I think her eyes are still closed. Her hands curl around the edge of the tub, white-knuckled and tight-gripped, and her flushed, petal-strewn chest heaves. She's squeezing my fingers in slippery flutters, and I suddenly wish I were in the bath with her, or that she were out here with me, or that I could at least see her face...but I can't deny I like this too. Making her come like a servant might, like it's just part of her bath, part of her nightly ritual.

She softens slowly, her head still turned away. The fire pops. When she lifts her hands, fresh rose petals, dark as the night sky, fall from the edge of the tub into the water.

I stare at them as they float and swirl on the surface, like miniature boats. My fingers are still gripped by her, and it occurs to me with a blast of dizzy wonder that I just fucked someone who can conjure flower petals from thin air. Someone whose lungs and blood-pink ribs are visible to the naked eye.

That she's a queen too somehow seems like the most normal part of it all—although fingering royalty isn't exactly a common occurrence for me either.

I slide my hand free and, without thinking, lift it to my

mouth. A habit as old as sex, and I think nothing of it, although when she turns her head and watches me do it, her expression turns ardent. Like I've just done something that thrills her to her core.

She tastes perfect—sweet, sour, salt, an entire meal with dessert after. There's a hint of rose too, but as I keep sucking my fingers, the taste changes. And now it tastes like how the air smells—like electric sex, electric hope. Like a long-ago version of myself who dreamed and hoped and lusted without restraint.

And before I can even decipher *how* pussy can taste anything like that, the world floods itself with magic. Suddenly, like a gate has pulled up and dizzy, heady *everything* is sluicing into the room as if the room were a rose-lined bowl. The fire is brighter, citrine and scarlet and even a deep, deep blue. The autumn moon burns like a dark red sun through the window. The stars are brighter than I've ever seen them, and there's more of them than I've ever seen, so many more, and the Milky Way is a mottled, glowing smear through it all.

I look back to the queen, and she is—she is *luminescent*, a mysterious burn like the moon outside, at once cool and light-giving. Her eyes are the darkness that the night sky no longer is with its glut of stars, and her mouth is the shape of all my wild and secret thoughts.

And why have I made them secret? I am sitting next to a glistening queen in her castle, my fingers still in my mouth, my mind blowing wide open, and all I can think is: *Why?*

Why have I been pressing myself into the shape of someone easy, someone composed and guarded and temperate, when I'm none of those things? When I don't even really want to be? When what I really want is to be as hungry as I can be, as messy as I can be, as *much*?

When what I really want is someone or someplace insatiable for my insatiability?

And god, I've never been hungrier than I am right now—and yet never have I felt this sated, this alive. Is this what fairy sex is like? Why didn't this happen in the hall, then, with Maynard and Idalia?

And what does it matter when the queen is the most beautiful thing I've ever seen and all I need to do is lick every drop of water from her skin until she lets me have another taste of her directly from the source?

"Janneth," the queen says. Her voice is musical, a full song when she speaks, and I can't believe I didn't hear it before.

It's a lonely song—wind on the hills, a single deer in the trees—but it's the most exquisite sound I've ever heard.

She's moved forward in the tub while I've been staring at her with my fingers in my mouth. She rises, and then her hands are on me, her arms are around me, and I'm being hauled against her as her mouth crushes into mine. My fingers are still between us, and her tongue flickers over my knuckles, the thin web between forefinger and middle finger, making me moan. I feel her tongue on my fingers like I'd feel it on my cunt, and then when she impatiently yanks my hand down and her tongue slides freely against mine, the surge of need between my legs steals my inhales and exhales.

I press eagerly against her, even as her wet body soaks my thin robe, even with the tub between us, and I find her waist with my hands and search for her hips, and then I—

She pulls back, pressing a finger to my mouth because I'm chasing her kiss, chasing her, needing more. I feel crazed with it, and if she won't let me kiss her again, I think I might die.

"Pet," she murmurs, the edge of her mouth curling a little.

I answer with a grin, a wide, happy grin, because I'm so *happy* right now, in a way I haven't been for the past few years. The world is beautiful and she is beautiful, and I'm here, and everything tastes and smells and sounds like magic and hidden things.

She looks down at my robe—completely see-through now—and runs an idle finger over the erect tip of my nipple over the wet fabric. "We should get you to bed," she says.

"As long as it's your bed," I say, giving her my best pouty face—which doesn't last long, because I break into a disbelieving smile right after. I can't believe that I feel more like myself, here, captive in a mushroom and stag castle, than I did in Edinburgh while building a respectable and interesting career.

She makes a noise. It's almost like a laugh inside her chest, but it never leaves her mouth. Instead, she stands, takes her towel, and knots it securely around herself. She steps gracefully out of the tub and then takes my hand to raise me to my feet.

"If my bed is what you want, you shall have it," she says as seriously as a monarch giving a royal decree. "Come."

I follow her, floating on my feet, ready to follow her everywhere. I feel like the whole world is mine to take a bite out of, like my entire life is ready to be plucked and eaten on the spot.

And then somehow I'm already lying in her bed, my wet robe long gone, cloud-soft blankets pulled up to my chin. It's like I'm stoned—or drunk—because time seems to slip again, and then the queen is in bed next to me, her face next to mine. Her breath is sweet, and all over again, my body rouses.

Before tonight, I would have made sure to keep close to the edge of the bed, I would have tried to keep my body small, my breathing light. I would have waited until my lover fell asleep and then I would have snuck out, not wanting to seem too needy by asking for another round of sex or staying the whole night.

And that's if I even got into their bed at all—I've gotten very skilled at the quick-and-easy hookups over the past two years. One and done, in and out, on to the next. That way I never burn through someone's attraction to me, through their patience, through my own self-respect.

But whatever I'm feeling right now, worry about being small and easy is the least of it.

Whatever you do, I shall find pleasing, because you are mine.

And so I don't stop myself from inching even closer, from reaching for her.

She lets me kiss her and stroke her, and held tight in her arms, I lose track of time, until I can barely keep my eyes open. I never want to stop kissing her, though. I want to kiss her until I die.

"You will need rest for the hunt tomorrow," she tells me, pulling away.

"Can't we stay in bed all day?" I ask, because why not.

Another noise from her chest again. That almost laugh. "No. The ruler of the Stag Court hunts every Samhain. It's a tradition I cannot break."

I sigh unhappily. I don't particularly want to be tramping around the wet Highlands this late in the year. Some things just sound *cold*.

But when I realize the alternative is being away from the queen, my chest aches, like the organs inside it are trying to push free.

So to the hunt I will go.

I force my eyes open enough to resettle the covers around me and then nestle into her. She allows it, although there's something tentative in the way she does. Like this isn't typical fairy queen behavior, the after-fuck cuddle. "How is it still dark outside?" I murmur sleepily, smashing my face into her shoulder and rooting until I'm comfortable.

"You might remember I said days and nights move differently than in your world," she says. "To you, these next two

SIERRA SIMONE

days will feel longer. All the more reason you should sleep now."

And as much as I need to kiss her again, taste her again, stare wide-eyed at a sky that's alien in its glittering, bright bustle, I can't argue with her. With the scent of roses and magic in my nose, I fall fast asleep.

CHAPTER 9

I wake not in the queen's bed but in my own, blinking up at a canopy embroidered with black roses and bone-white antlers. The indifferent light of dawn stretches through the window, which means it should be early, but I feel as if I've slept an embarrassingly long amount of time. Like I've slept the first hard, real sleep I've had since jumping feet-first into the sausage grinder of grad student life.

Even so, when I sit up and swing my feet out of bed, I still feel floaty, bright and aware and *hungry*.

Not for food, though. Not at all.

But my eagerness to get back to the queen is forestalled when I see the tub in the middle of my room has been replaced with a table. It's carved and fashioned in the shape of a doe dipping her head to drink, and on her wooden back rests a plate of warm bread and fluffy butter, a bowl of mixed berries and cream, and a steaming cup of tea. A note written in dark red ink is propped against the teacup.

You may not see me until you've eaten. Don't forget salt.

—M

M. It can only be her, which means that can only be her initial. Her name starts with *M.*

I guess a few possible names as I find the salt—Marian, Margaret, Myrtle—and sprinkle a few grains on each of the breakfast items. Maybe I could get the queen's name today—or whatever it is she'd like to be called, in light of the fairies' wariness around true names. I yearn to call her something more intimate than *Your Majesty.* Even if the whole *Your Majesty* thing is a little hot.

And the need to see her is like a leash tugging on my neck, and how would she know if I'd eaten anyway? Maybe I could just eat a bite or two, so that it wouldn't be lying if I said I ate *some* breakfast, and then I could go find her right away...

I take a bite of bread and butter with salt sprinkled on top, and it's the best bread I've ever eaten, and so I take another bite, and another, and by the time I've finished, I feel suddenly more solid. Less floaty. Like I'm sobering up, although I wasn't even drunk last night.

The world is sober now too. The low fire in my fireplace is a normal fire; the dawn sky outside is beautiful, but the same beauty I've known my entire life. And my searing need to see the queen...

Well, it's still there, but at least I can think other thoughts too. Think logically about things. Does salt help with thinking clearly, along with keeping me ready to go back to the mortal world?

Weird.

The wardrobe provides yet again: thick hose with suede patches inside the knees, a green dress made of a fine wool and split up the skirt for easy riding, and a warm cloak the gold-yellow of birch leaves in autumn.

After I dress, I make use of the small water closet to the side of the room and the toothbrush and toothpaste left for me near the small jug of water and basin. They are unmistakably new, unmistakably *mortal*, still in their packages, and I wonder if they keep a supply of such things for all their mortal guests or if this is something procured just for me.

I also wonder if fairies need toothpaste at all. If they don't, it fits with the whole being-immortal-and-preternaturally-beautiful thing, but still. It hardly seems fair.

On a whim, I slip my phone into the pocket of my dress before I leave the room. Just in case there's a signal out in the wilderness, although that's literally never been the case near the dig site, and also I'm not actually *in* Scotland anymore. At least I think not? I put *learn how Faerie fits into the fabric of known universe* on my mental to-do list and then venture forth to find the queen.

"YOUR MAJESTY KNOWS THE NECESSITY. Especially given what's happened with the Dark Druid...we can't afford for anything else to go wrong."

"Not if I find another way," comes the queen's voice in reply. It's colder and harder than I've heard it before, and that's including the time she forced the servant from the Thistle Court to endure his own lady's trick. "I expect your support in this, Sholto."

I round the corner into the banquet hall—the ever-helpful castle leaves settling to the floor as I walk inside—and see the queen sitting on her throne, with Felipe, Morven, and a tall, gray-skinned man I don't recognize in front of her. Sholto, I presume.

They don't notice me at first, continuing to argue as I walk toward the stag throne with its menacing web of antlers arcing up behind the queen's dark head. She's wearing breeches and a tunic made of a sturdy red wool, with high leather boots and a knife already belted at her hip. Her hair is gathered in a thick plait draped over one shoulder, and the only nod to her royal station, aside from the throne where she sits, is a heavy gold ring on her left hand.

"Your Majesty," Sholto attempts again, "there is no other way. If there were, don't you think one of the courts of Elphame would have found it long before now?"

"There is another way, which you know well," the queen says, turning the ring slowly on her finger. "It only has to be chosen."

Morven gives a low, bitter laugh at that. "Chosen indeed."

Felipe looks pale, but he doesn't speak.

"But it should not be chosen," Sholto says, sounding a little desperate now. "This is the way Samhain is done—the way the Shadow Market is closed—and the way things have been done since the first Cernunnos walked these hills. It is a law that cannot be gainsaid, no matter what we wish."

The queen's expression remains cold, stony. "Perhaps no one has tried hard enough to gainsay it."

"Your Majesty," pleads Sholto, "even the Thistle Court did their duty the last time. This is what being a fae ruler *is*. This is the most secret, and most sacred, act a fae ruler must *do*, and the Thistle Queen did her job admirably—"

"I do not wish to hear what the Thistle Queen did," snaps the queen.

"You should," Morven says irritably. "She has held her court with strength—"

"And sly violence," the queen says. "I would not be like her."

"Our own mother made a habit of sly violence, if you don't recall," Morven retorts. "Do you not remember the assassinations? The wars? The curses? The druid she cursed is still suffering, still bound, two years after her death. But you can't argue that she didn't keep our court strong and safe. That she didn't do her duty when it was asked of her."

The queen frowns but doesn't answer.

Sholto cuts in. "Duty aside, I promise you I can find you a hundred mortals more pleasing—"

He breaks off and turns around, seeming to realize just now that I'm here. He glares at me.

I smile at him. "More pleasing than me? Because I have it on good authority that I'm very pleasing."

Felipe clears his throat and looks to the floor. Morven rolls his eyes.

The queen, for her part, says nothing. But there is something like a smile on her lips.

Sholto sputters. "This is a council meeting! Which you were not invited to, nor are you privy to the matters we must discuss. I insist you leave—"

"The council meeting is adjourned," says the queen, standing up and closing the matter. "It's time for our hunt. And Sholto, I recommend you adjust your expectations about what Janneth is privy to. She'll be by my side until Third Night. Yes," she adds at Sholto's mutinous expression, "even at the treaty negotiations tomorrow."

This is the first I've heard of any treaty or its negotiations, but if it gets me one over on this Sholto asshole, then treaty negotiations are my new favorite thing. I give him a smug look, and he returns it with a fuming one of his own—which is cut short when the queen steps off the dais and he and the others sink into their obeisances. I kneel too, but the queen touches my shoulder.

"Come, Janneth. We have a hunt to ready for."

CHAPTER 10

The whole court, it seems, is out for the hunt, including Felipe, Morven, Idalia, and Maynard, but not Sholto. I don't know if this is because Sholto is cranky about me being near the queen, or if he's not really the outdoorsy type. He does give off big "reading spy reports by candlelight" energy, so maybe it's the latter.

But it's hard to worry about Sholto when the day is like something out of a story—misty and moody, bright orange and yellow leaves dripping, the gray sky so low that the hills scrape against it, carding away scraps of cloud like wool. And the queen is upright and magnetic on her white horse, her braid bouncing on her shoulder as she leads the party from the castle at a trot.

Though she made sure I'm atop a horse (that I sort of know how to ride, thanks to a few weekends at Alfie's country pile in Buckinghamshire) and that I'm equipped with a crossbow (that I have no idea how to shoot), she's been whisked away by one person or another since the hunting party began to gather, to the point where the entire crowd now separates us.

I hate it. I feel like I'm in high school again. I want to be next to her, and at the same time, I'm terrified of being close to her, and it's not the terror of knowing she can make rose petals flutter from thin air or knowing she'll happily watch someone bleed at her feet. It's the terror of wanting someone so much that it feels like my bones are about to punch their way out of my skin.

I stay at the back of the party, riding slowly down the sloping lane to the forest, where the real action will happen. I scan the terrain as I go, a distant voice reminding me that if I were to escape, this would be the ideal situation. If I hang back at the next twist in the road, if I wait until we're scattered in the trees...

But then what? I somehow make it back to the mortal world without any help? I mean, I'm pretty sure we came through the tomb last night, but I don't know *how*. I don't know how Maynard could use the tomb as a way into Faerie when I've been inside it hundreds and hundreds of times and never saw anything but dirt and stone and darkness.

And that's assuming I can find the tomb at all. The shape of the hills around the castle vaguely matches with what I know from my world, but everything is *more* here. Taller, steeper, craggier. The valleys and lowlands aren't the nearly bare grasslands and fields they are back home but are covered in old-growth forest burning in the colors of autumn. From the castle, I thought I'd seen a loch and the silver line of the sea, but I'm almost certain we're headed east, away from the water, and now that I'm down in the trees, the strangeness and largeness of Faerie is disorienting.

Only the narrow, half-sunken way through the forest provides any sort of clue where we're going—and as the lane grows twistier and the trees arching overhead hide more and more of the sky, those clues evaporate.

Even if I managed to get away, I'd be lost. Lost in a place

where I still don't know all the rules, lost in a place where I can't trust someone not to haul me right back to the Stag Court.

But I could stay. Stay here, with the queen.

It's only one more day after today, I reassure myself. A long-ass fairy day, maybe, but still. If I hang out here until tomorrow night, then I have the queen's promise she'll let me go, and I'll be back in my world and none the worse for wear. *Better* for wear, really, if I consider all the good sex I've had, all the beautiful and curious things I've seen, including getting to see one of de Segovia's companions in the flesh and solving the mystery of the missing castle.

And if the idea of leaving and never seeing the queen again makes something knot tight in my chest, then that doesn't matter. It's not like it changes anything. It's a good bargain, and that's that.

"I wouldn't, if you're thinking about it," someone says in Latin from beside me, and I turn to see Felipe. He's hung back too, riding next to me at my beginner's pace.

"Wouldn't what? Escape into a mysterious forest that's maybe full of monsters?" I say, sliding him a smile.

He seems a little startled by my easiness, and then he frowns. "I take it you tasted fruit last night."

I flush a little to remember that he probably saw me in full Janneth panoply last night. I've done some brazen things before but usually among other brazen people. Not in front of solemn-eyed, should-be-dead Spanish gentry.

He must see my expression, because he says, almost gently, "This is an unchaste place. I do not think less of anyone for what they do here. But at any rate, I do not mean what you did in the court. I'm thinking you went to someone's bed afterward."

Ahead of us, I can make out the form of the queen, only visible now and again as the riders in front of me move and shift. She's riding next to Morven—predictably all in black—and he seems to be saying something she's not thrilled with, judging by her tense posture.

The glimpses I catch of her thighs on either side of her saddle arrest me.

"Ah," Felipe says, following my gaze. "The queen. Heady fruit indeed, then."

It takes its time becoming clear, but once it does, the truth feels as obvious as a standing stone in the middle of a moor.

Fruit. *Tasting*. The salt this morning.

"The fruit isn't fruit," I say. I feel suddenly very, very human and dumb.

"No." It's his turn to flush, looking down at his reins for a moment. "It's everything of a fairy's body—sweat, tears, the taste of their mouths. But in some...versions...it's more potent."

"Sex," I state, remembering sucking my fingers clean next to the queen's bath.

"Yes."

I wonder how fairies aren't stoned all the fucking time, then. Kissing? Orgies? They have to be "eating" fairy fruit constantly.

Felipe seems to know what I'm thinking, because he adds, "It doesn't affect the fairies nearly as much as it affects mortals. It's more like wine to them. Only in its most concentrated form does it approach what mortals feel after lying in a fairy's bed."

"Wait. Sex isn't the most concentrated?"

"Blood is the most potent," Felipe says with a flat kind of finality, and I remember the revelers dragging their fingers through the Thistle courtier's blood last night. I shiver.

Ahead of us, I see Morven turned fully toward the queen, as if trying to convince her of something, and I see her shake her head. The short, curt shake of someone saying no.

Morven jerks his reins and wheels away, thundering back down the line of riders with his face set in a murderous expression. When he passes me and Felipe, he gives me a look like he'd happily throw me into a pit of alligators, and then he's gone.

"He hates her," Felipe says quietly, after Morven is long past us.

"Why?" I look ahead at the queen, who's still riding with a proud, impeccable seat. She's imperious, yes, with a streak of cruelty that can't be denied, but it doesn't seem out of place here in Faerie. Not to the point where it would earn a sibling's hatred.

"There's a prophecy about the Nightglass twins," Felipe says. "Morven and her. That since they were born under the same stars, to the same powerful queen, great rulers they both could grow to be, but the throne of the Stag Court will only know a single Nightglass. She took the crown upon her mother's death, which means Morven will never be ruler here. And he's never forgiven anyone for it, though he is more blessed than he thinks. Following in his mother's footsteps in no small feat, as his mother was strong, feared, and cruel. Deeply cruel by Seelie standards, I suppose, but her cruelty kept the Stag Court first among the courts of the folk. The new queen is struggling, I think, to hold the other courts at bay."

"Like the Thistle Court?" I ask.

Felipe nods. "Their lady is also a great queen, but as an Unseelie queen, she has no limit to what she'll do for chaos or for power. I think..." He pauses for a moment. "I think our new queen is finding she *does* have limits. But they are not limits permitted to true rulers of Elphame, not if they want to keep their people safe."

"You called her and Morven the Nightglass twins," I say. "Is that their name? Like a family name?"

"It is *a* name. They were born partly glassed," Felipe says, as if that's a thing I should know about. "I'm sure you saw when you were, ah, *with* the queen last night."

I think of her clear back, the red and pink of her muscles and lungs and bone. Delicate and hale, all at once. And there for the entire world to see, something that's the most private of things. The living insides of her.

Glassed.

"Morven has to be more careful of his glass," Felipe tells me. "If he is unclothed, you can see straight to his heart."

No wonder he's careful to always wear black—no gauzy, ruffly shirts for Morven. For him, guarding his heart might be more literal than any mortal can ever imagine.

I think of his bitter laugh in the hall earlier. "What were you talking about?" I ask Felipe as I dodge a branch hanging low over the road. "In the hall when I came in."

Felipe gives me a small smile, but his answer is blunt. "You," he says.

"Me?" I'd guessed as much given Sholto's *a hundred mortals* remark, but I don't like the sound of this at all.

"There is a tradition of keeping mortals here in Faerie," he explains. "Against their will. It's a very old thing, that kind of keeping. Mortals are beloved in Faerie, and treated well, as you can see from me and my long life. But not every mortal is ready for it—only the bravest and most creative, I think."

My pride prickles a little at that, as if he's just issued a challenge. "Were you ready for it?" I ask. "Were you willing?"

"I was," he says. And there's a certainty in his voice that pokes a quick hole in my umbrage. I can't deny I'm quickly becoming infatuated with the queen, and I can't deny Faerie is the only place I've been that seems like a match for my appetites—not just carnal but intellectual too. A world that can meet my curiosity with layer after layer of magic.

But it's dangerous too, and alien, and no matter how sexy

the queen is when she's calling me her pet, I don't think I could stay forever. Right?

That would be bananas. I have a whole life back home. With eye-watering amounts of student loan debt. With a love life that's at turns nonexistent and depressing. With friends I keep at arm's length and a vocation that seems ready to disillusion me at a moment's notice.

"It doesn't matter," I say, convincing myself as much as him. "The queen promised I'd be able to go home tomorrow."

"Well, then," Felipe says, "the matter is settled anyway."

"Right," I say, and then we ride along in relative silence, with only the breeze rippling through the forest and the chatter of the fairies to break it.

CHAPTER 11

Felipe told me what to expect from the hunt, but it still catches me by surprise when the hunt master blows her whistle and the staghounds explode from her side, charging into the trees and fanning out to find the deer.

With a jerk of her reins, the queen follows the hounds, the hunt master close by her side, the rest of the court following at various paces ranging from fast to sauntering. That too, Felipe had prepared me for, because a hunt is first and foremost a disport, and most of the riders will mill about and gossip until the cold and damp grows tiresome, and then they'll relocate to the pavilion erected in the forest and mill about and gossip there instead.

Only the queen and the hunt master will be hard on our prey, and even then, there is no certainty they will stay together in pursuit of it. A hunt at the Court of Stags seems to be half parade, half the queen off by herself in the woods. And looking at the woods—gold birch, red rowan, carpeted in bronze and green ferns—I can't blame her.

SIERRA SIMONE

Somehow I lose Felipe in the charge and then get turned around enough that I lose sight of most of the court too. My horse, chosen for its patience and docility, is more than happy to plod aimlessly through the trees, and after a while, I give up trying to find the rest of the riders and focus on trying to make it back to the road. If I can find the road, I can find the castle... or even try to find the tomb and a possible doorway back into my own life.

I immediately dismiss the thought. I made a bargain, and even if bargains with kidnapping queens don't count, I still want to keep this one. Especially if it means being the queen's pet for another day.

We tromp through the ferns, weave between trees, periodically stop as I strain my ears for the hunt master's whistle or the chatter of the courtiers, but there is nothing. Nothing but the cool, damp air and the trees fluttering and the occasional huff from my horse when I change direction.

I'm starting to panic that I'm lost in a fairy forest—something that's never good for people in the stories—when I see another horse standing under a large oak, riderless and patient.

I know immediately it's the queen's. The other horses in the hunt are silver or gold, with ribbons and flowers braided into their manes and tails.

The queen's horse is unadorned, its coat a dark red that reminds me of the color of her lungs.

If it's here, then she must be too.

I somehow manage to dismount my own horse—clumsily, it must be said—and it obediently ambles over to the queen's and begins nosing the ground for food. And with the feeling of being lost still tugging at my mind, I look for the queen, searching an ever-wider radius around our horses, until I finally catch sight of red wool and raven-dark hair.

The queen is standing between two slender birches with her crossbow drawn and raised, her finger not yet on the trigger. At her hip is the dagger I saw this morning, along with a quiver full of bolts and a silver goat's foot lever for drawing the weapon's string.

There's no one else around, not even the hunt master. And there's no sign of the hounds.

The queen doesn't speak as I step closer, but she does take a small step to the side, allowing me to stand next to her.

I know enough to be still, to be as silent as I can, but I will never be as still and silent as the queen, who's as motionless as her throne, as the hill the castle is carved from. Her gloved hands are completely steady; her pulse jumps in her neck.

And then I hear it. The rustle and crush of the stag moving through the trees, subtle at first, and then more and more obvious as it gets closer, as I can clearly make out its thick, multipoint antlers, its onyx eyes. It's coming to drink from a small burn that runs through the woods here, and I feel the queen shift ever so slightly as it dips its head to drink.

I've seen deer before, of course, and as a girl from the American Midwest, I grew up knowing plenty of hunters who exclusively hunted deer, but it's still shocking to see the stag up close, majestic, heedless, innocent, and know it's marked for death. That every second might be its last. Even the forest seems shocked—a heavy hush filling the air, a feeling like the world is holding its breath, caught between life and inevitable death.

The queen doesn't miss when she shoots. The drawstring snaps, and the bolt sinks into the stag's neck, deep and clean. It makes a choked noise—a wounded sound that cuts me to hear—and then staggers to the side, collapsing first onto its forelegs, and then all the way onto its side, its ribs heaving and blood running from its neck.

The queen lowers her crossbow and looks for a moment. Breathes.

"Come," she says quietly to me and then makes her silent way over to the stag, which is still alive, but barely.

She kneels in front of the dying beast, as do I, and she pulls her goatskin gloves off with her teeth. Her naked hand goes to its fur, and her eyes close for a moment. When she opens them, I realize their eyes are the exact same pitch of glittering onyx.

"Thank you," the queen says to her victim, pressing her forehead to its head. Her voice is solemn, trembling a little at the edges of her words. Her hand drops to the knife at her hip as she speaks. "Thank you."

The stag breathes out, almost like a sigh, and then goes entirely still. Animal to object in the space of an instant. The dagger glints in the silver light of the forest as the queen straightens once more. I think I see a single tear caught on her lashes as she does, but then I can only see her in profile as she moves to the side of the deer, her hand bracing on the deer's chest as she swiftly, expertly, begins cutting its chest open.

I watch, fascinated, as she opens the deer up, layer by layer, like she's unstitching a doll. First its hide with quick, precise flicks, exposing the ruddy muscle underneath. And then its sternum, which she saws through with the serrated back of the knife as easily as I might saw through a loaf of fresh bread. And then she pries the animal's chest apart with her bare hands, revealing something as intimate as what I saw when I looked at her glassed back. The beautiful clockwork of a being, caged and padded with bone and muscle.

The heart rests inside, a heavy fruit, and the queen reaches inside and plucks it from the chest. When she pulls her hand free, blood shines on her wrist and fingers and ring. With another deft flick of her knife, she cuts open the sac covering the organ, and then, dropping the knife to the leaf-covered ground below, she peels the heart of its caul like an orange. What's left behind is mauve, wet, tender looking.

Blood drips between her long fingers as she lifts it to her lips and takes a bite. A big one, her white teeth sinking into the soft flesh of the heart and leaving behind a small concavity in the shape of her mouth. Blood smears her lips, runs down her chin, and she looks at me with feral, flashing eyes, and I should be horrified, I should hate this, I should be afraid.

Horror is the last thing I feel.

She offers me the heart, the way a lover might offer a sip of wine from their glass, and I look back up at her blood-smeared face, I think of the blood on the hem of my gown last night, I think of her cunt around my fingers and the petals falling from her hands and the gruesomely lovely expanse of her back.

I'm not *becoming* infatuated at all; I'm already infatuated and then some.

I barely know the queen at all, I don't even know her name, and yet kneeling with her in the forest, her bloody hand offering me a bite of raw heart, I think I know everything I need to know.

I take the heart from her hands and lift it to my mouth. It's still warm, and heavier than I think it will be, and *soft*. Softer than steak. Blood drips onto the leaves and crushed ferns underneath me as I take a long breath, smelling the metallic tang of fresh blood. And then I take a bite, having to pull to tear it free.

It's tender between my teeth, and it tastes like blood, and it's shockingly delicious. Like a rare cut of meat, like tartare at a fancy restaurant. And for a moment, long and lingering, I taste something more than meat, more than blood.

I taste the forest. I taste *here*. Faerie. History and magic and cruelty and wonder and depth.

I taste what I wanted to taste my entire life, until I made myself stop wanting it.

I swallow the heart meat and then lift my eyes to the queen's. Her stare is shining with something I don't understand, but I don't have to wonder for long. She takes the heart from my hands and sets it carefully on a pillow of ferns. And then her bloody hands are twisted in my dress, dragging me close to her for a hard, crushing kiss.

She tastes of blood and, past that, like she did last night, like lust and hope and promises I've broken to myself only to find that someone else was keeping them for me.

She tastes like fairy fruit. And I choose each and every lick of it.

I open more to her searching tongue, melting against her as it strokes against mine, flickers, devours. Our lips are slippery with blood, and when she lifts a hand to hold my face in place for her pleasure, I feel the blood on my jaw and on my cheek.

The entire world is inside of me and inside of her, and between our mouths is the truth of living, dying, wanting.

The truth is that I want to swallow it all whole, come what may.

I hear the excited baying of the hounds and then the whistle of the hunt master, very close, and the queen breaks off our kiss. Through the dizzy fruit feeling, I'm gratified to see she looks very annoyed at the interruption.

"Your Majesty," the hunt master says, sounding out of breath as she kneels. "Well shot."

"Thank you," the queen says, rising easily to her feet and then helping me up with firm fingers wrapped around my hand. The dogs sit obediently near the hunt master, but their noses work with avid intensity, smelling the deer and the spilled blood. "I trust you'll make sure our prize is ready for the feast tonight?"

"I will, Your Majesty," the hunt master says, already pulling out her own knife to dress the deer. "Would you like me to save the rest of the heart for the others?"

"Yes." The queen smiles sharply. "Morven shall have the

rest. And will you have someone see to our horses as well? I think we'll take the long way to the pavilion."

"Yes, Your Majesty," answers the hunt master, and after stopping by her horse to sling a bag over her shoulder, the queen leads me away from the stag and deeper into the forest.

CHAPTER 12

I don't know how long we walk, not only because the fruit of the queen's kiss is sweet in my blood but because the sun doesn't move across the sky in the same way here, and so what feels like an hour might only be a few minutes in fairy time. But we stop by the burn, which is shallower and wider here, and wash with rose-scented soap from the queen's bag.

After the blood is cleaned from our hands and faces, the queen gives me a leather costrel of water to drink, and then when I'm done, she runs a thumb along the edge of my lower lip to catch a stray drop of water.

Her eyes are as hot as they were when she was kissing me with the heart between us, and the answering heat inside me arrows straight to my clit. An ache—hot and full—throbs along the narrow length to the small, needy glans, and my entire pussy responds.

Just from her stare.

"Would you like me to be your pet now?" I whisper. It doesn't even occur to me to be shy about it, to try to hide how much I want her. Or to hide how much I want her to want me back. I could blame it on the fruit, of course, and pretend I'm too stoned to keep up the pretense of Easy Janneth, but I won't.

Even without the fruit earlier today, I felt the same—like keeping hold of that flimsy, colorless version of myself had become impossible overnight. Impossible once she told me that everything I did would be pleasing to her.

And she seems pleased now, or at least aroused, because her eyes flash as she leans in to kiss me again, and her hands are demanding, eager, pulling me close and then finding my hips, my ass, my breasts. "Yes," says the queen finally, shoving up my dress to curl her fingers over my clothed pussy. "Now. Always."

I moan into her kiss as she plunders my mouth and then give a surprised exhale when she pushes me onto my back. I'm cushioned by ferns and leaves, and so it's not at all uncomfortable, only a bit cool and damp, and that's no bother when I'm running so hot all over.

She's kneeling over me with her knife once again in her hand.

I have a moment of cold, clear worry, which simmers into something so molten I can't help squirming as she slides the point against the soft fabric of her breeches and then cuts them open with an impatient flick. She tosses the knife aside and tears the fabric even farther apart so that her sex is bared to the open air.

She moves over me, swinging her knee easily over my head so she can straddle my face. She reaches down to drag her fingers to my chin, parting my lips, and then she lowers herself to fuck my open mouth.

I'm not prepared—could never have been prepared—for the unmediated taste of her. Sweet and warm, almost citrusy. With that deep flavor only pussy has. And then, just as with her kiss, just as last night, there is the taste under the taste, and if her kisses were enough to get me stoned, then licking her cunt is enough to send me *flying*.

I feel every thread of life around me, every breath and whisper of stirring leaves and searching tendril of mycelium. I feel *her*, strong, hot, the muscles in her thighs and hips quivering, her blood rich as an entire universe in her veins. I feel *myself*: the quick pants swelling my lungs, and the twist in my belly, and the restless kick of my legs as my body searches for friction that isn't there.

And then, as I pull her erect clit into my mouth, I realize I can feel *her* pleasure too, like we're connected, like the sensation shivering through her is universal, radiating out from her and into the rest of the world, and with a cry against her flesh, I climax with a shuddering seize, without having even touched myself once.

I buck and writhe underneath her, the orgasm too hard to bear, because it's not just in my body, but in my *mind*, like all of me is releasing, clenching, releasing, and though it's hard to see anything but torn breeches and scarlet tunic and flashes of the gold leaves, I know she must like this, that this pleases her, because she stabs a hand into my hair and rides my face like she paid for it. Or bargained for it, at least.

I'm no stranger to having a lover sit on my face, but no one has ever done it like the queen is doing now, giving me so much of her weight, her hand twisting hard in my hair to give herself enough leverage to fuck my mouth with short, sharp rocks of her hips. I feel pinned, used, blissed out as fuck, and I can't get enough of her even as the fading orgasm still ripples through my cunt. Each taste is another blow to my sanity, each new rush of slickness is the end of everything I ever knew and the beginning of everything I ever wanted.

And it occurs to me, with the fairy queen hot and wet on my face, with my back against the damp forest floor, that the reason I'm not more afraid, that I'm not miserable despite being literally kidnapped, is that I think I might fit here. Some-how. Nonsensically.

Because when everything else is so outrageous, so danger-ously indulgent, when everything around me is also *too much*, I don't feel like I'm too much at all. I feel like I'm just the right amount.

The queen's thighs tense around my head, she gives a sharp, punched exhale, and then she orgasms against my mouth, which I know mostly from the hard quiver of her thighs and the rough grunts she makes as she fucks my mouth through it all.

My body answers again, a softer climax than the first but powerful nonetheless, and when she finally goes still, she reaches back and impatiently rucks up my dress so she can slide her hand into the front of my hose. She doesn't stroke me, it's too perfunctory a touch for that—more like she wants to see how wet I am.

She makes a satisfied noise when she finds me dripping and then gets to her feet. Rose petals fall from her hands as she does; I can feel them tangled in my hair. I lay dazed on the ground, blinking up at the silver sky through the gold and red leaves, already pining for the taste of her again and not knowing if she'll let me have it.

"Janneth," the queen says, and I look at where she's settled herself under a large oak, her legs crossed. She licks me off her fingers as fastidiously as a cat might clean its paw.

I get to my hands and knees, and she beckons me forward. I crawl, even though she hasn't asked it of me, because I think she might like it and because I know I will.

And she does like it, I think, because her chest is moving with barely controlled breaths and her mouth is parted, like someone's set a feast in front of her.

"Come closer," she says, voice low and songlike, and I crawl into her lap and straddle her. The queen wastes no time in shoving her hand down my hose once more, and she finds the heart of me right away. The first slide of her fingers against my clit has me looping my arms around her shoulders to support myself, and the second has me pressing my head to hers.

She angles her hand and pushes two fingers inside me—then three when she sees how easily I take two. She's not the kind for easy, I think, not the kind for gentle. She'd want to me to feel her after she's been someplace on my body, and I love that, I want that. I want to be marked, I want her to make me sore, because then every time I move or twist or sit, she'll be with me, the memory of this moment will still be alive.

"I want to eat you again," I breathe as she works her fingers inside of me. My face is against the side of hers; I smell the rose scent of her hair. I shudder as she curls her fingers inside me. "I want to taste you again. Please let me. Please let me."

"Oh, Janneth," she sighs, fully fucking me now. My legs can't go any wider; I'm resting my full weight on her hand. "That's the fruit talking."

"I don't care," I pant, because I don't, I don't. I desired her before the fruit, and I desired her after, and the only difference is in how dizzy and light and fantastic I feel now, and I'm so *hungry* for her, for the fruit, that I know why mortals died without it in the stories. Why they wasted away, keening for it, weeping for it.

If I don't get to lick her cunt again, I will simply die.

As if taking mercy on me, she offers me her mouth as I ride her hand, moving my hips so I can rub my clit against her palm, and the sweet, still slightly bloody taste of her mouth slakes the thirst somewhat, eases the urgent need inside, just in time for me to explode right there in her lap.

I cry out against her lips, my hands twisted in her tunic,

my entire body one big bowstring drawn taut and then released.

"That's right," she murmurs, giving my lip a swift bite and then licking away the sting. Bursts of pleasure bunch and flow around her touch, her breach of me. "That's it. You are so beautiful, Janneth, so beautiful always, but especially when you're coming for me."

Eventually, I can't even kiss her anymore, can't even move or think beyond the cataclysm erupting around her fingers and pouring bliss into every corner of my being. At some point, she's leaned back against the trunk of the tree, and my face has ended up in the crook of her neck, and I'm slumped totally against her, trembling and consumed.

"I want to know your name," I mumble. "I want to say it when we fuck."

I feel her considering this.

"Not your whole name or true name or whatever it's called," I say quietly. "Just something to call you. I love it when you say my name; I want to say yours so you can have that feeling too."

She goes still. I pull back a little to see her face, and I see her giving me the same expression she gave me in the bath, like I've surprised her beyond measure. Like her own reaction is surprising.

A muscle jumps in her jaw, and then she takes a breath. "Morgana," she says. Her fingers are still inside me. "My name is Morgana."

CHAPTER 13

Morgana feeds me salt from a small pouch in her bag, having me lick the grains off her fingertips, and she watches me as my head clears.

"I still want to lick your cunt," I tell her, utterly sober, and she laughs. It's the first real laugh I've heard from her—bright and bell-like, like the feeling of a blue Highland sky on a summer's day. The wide smile on her face almost hurts to look at, it's so dazzling.

"I'd be a bad host if I didn't give my guest what she wanted," Morgana says, and then she settles back against the tree, draws one knee up, and allows me to fall under the spell of the fairy fruit all over again.

I don't know how long in human time we stay there by the stream, kissing and fucking, since the day is suspended in silvery autumn light. But I do know I have to sleep for several long hours in the middle of it. I do know by the time she feeds me more salt and we walk back to the pavilion, my mouth is swollen and my pussy is sore. In my old life, it would feel like a walk of shame to enter the pavilioned feasting site with disheveled clothes and mussed hair, but since there are already several fairies fucking around us, there doesn't seem much to be ashamed about. Indeed, the queen herself strides into the camp with her torn breeches flapping around her thighs and a few stray leaves caught in her braid, and she seems no less regal for it.

We wash and change for the feast—me into a soft-pink gown held up with thin straps and stitched with crystals, her into a black silk dress with a plunging neckline and the pattern of thorns picked out in silver thread. It's strapless, with black ribbons crisscrossing down her arms, their silk tails tied at her wrists and draping all the way to the rug-covered ground of her pavilion. Her hair, freshly washed, dried, and wound up in an elaborate style, is set with her antler crown, and as usual, she wears no other ornament, save for her ring.

When she turns, I see the very beginnings of her glassed back peeping above her gown. Enough to draw attention, but not enough to be truly vulnerable, perhaps. I think of Morven having to hide his heart, and shudder. It would be a vulnerability anywhere, but here in Faerie? It's more like a curse.

The feast begins at twilight, right there under the low misty sky. Fires burn in a circle around us, and a glowing blue haze seems to fill the air, making the forest as well lit as the hall was last night, even as night comes. Trestle tables are arrayed in front of a temporary dais with two simple but heavy chairs atop it; already the tables are heaped with food: berries and hazelnuts and stuffed mushrooms, cakes made of oats and honey, glossy red apples, and meat pies with flaky golden crusts.

Neither Morven nor Sholto is here, but I see Maynard and Idalia thick in the fray and Felipe seated at a table near the dais. Together, Morgana and I sit and toast and feast. Together, we listen to Maynard sing us ballads; we watch courtiers dance reels and leaping, whirling waltzes; we watch as Morgana's stag, which has been roasting over an open fire, is carved and served.

I frequently catch Morgana looking at me like she's wondering when she can have me flat on my back again.

Finally the feast gets to the point where almost no one is looking to the queen anymore, because the merriment is so high and the fairies are all drunk or fucking (or both), and Morgana slips her hand into mine. "When I stand, follow me quickly," she says. "Let's not be seen."

I do as she says, and we slip into the shadows behind the dais before the rest of the court can mark our absence, although I notice Felipe watching us, his face solemn in the bonfire light.

She's smiling when we duck back into her personal pavilion, the light of the candelabra flickering along the high lines of her cheeks and casting shadows under her long lashes.

"I've never snuck away from my own court before," she confesses, standing in the middle of her tent and looking around like a kid who's just played hooky for the first time. "I feel a little giddy."

As someone who used to play hooky as often as I could get away with it, I have to laugh a little at her wonder. "It's pretty great," I say, and then I think of how responsible I've been for the past few years. "Even when it's a job you want to do, actually doing it can be exhausting sometimes."

Her fingertips drag across the table in the middle of the tent as she walks to a high-backed chair and sits. She pats the surface in front of her, indicating where I should sit, and *yes, please*. I hop up in front of her and make sure my skirts aren't trapped under my legs, just in case things get interesting.

She leans back in the chair and studies me with dark eyes. "Are you speaking from experience? About the job?"

Well. Yeah. "I've spent the last five years of my life fighting against time, money, and student visa renewals so I could learn to be an archaeologist," I explain. "But now that I'm on the brink of moving into the field for real, I sometimes wonder if I made a mistake." I pause and then sigh. "Actually, I started wondering if it was a mistake after the very first class I took."

She regards me. "Then why go on? Why not find something else?"

I don't know if I can answer that. At least not in any way that makes sense. "The past used to feel so magical to me," I say. "Which sounds stupid now that I'm here in a place where magic is real—but that's how it felt. Like there was this *mystery* just beckoning, and all I had to do was reach out my hand and part the veil, and I'd be inside it. As if the way the past made me feel was how the past would be like to study."

"And that wasn't the case."

I brace my feet on either side of her chair, the hem of my dress falling into her lap, crystals against thorns. "Archaeology sometimes has this way of reducing everything to the most pragmatic version of itself. There's very little room for feeling and fantasy in what's supposed to be a science. And even though I still love it—and even though it feels like the one thing in my life that has an appetite to match my own—it's bleeding me dry of who I used to be. Eventually everything will be small and recordable and quantifiable and contained, and that will be that. And sometimes I'm afraid that this is how everything is in the world—that any person, hobby, or place is a mirage about to disappear. You think you love something, you think it will love you back, but then the closer you get, the further it draws away from you. The more you realize that, rather than the thing itself, you loved the way it made you feel when you knew nothing about it instead."

I suddenly feel very depressed.

The queen puts her elbow on the arm of the chair and then props her head on her hand. It's a more informal pose than I've ever seen from her, forest sex aside, and I like it. It makes her look arrogant, a little disdainful, and it's very hot.

"As to archaeology, why is it the only magic left in your life?" she asks. "Not counting your time here, of course."

I push my face in my hands. "It's embarrassing to talk about," I mumble into my palms.

"I like embarrassing," she says. "I like uncomfortable."

I look at her through my splayed fingers, and she looks back at me, entirely seriously.

"I mean it, Janneth. Some lovers might enjoy gifts of jewels and gold, others might want ballads or praise, but I have no need of those things. Instead, I want to see inside you. I want every ugly secret and thwarted hope; I want whatever makes you flush and squirm and hate yourself at night. I suppose it might be because, in the most literal sense, people have always been able to see inside me, but it could just as easily be that I'm more than a little sadistic. Whatever the reason, you need not treat your humiliations as things that will diminish what I feel for you. Your trust in showing them to me will feed me, delight me, because you delight me. It is like seeing your heart naked, or your mind naked, and I think as I've established earlier today, I like seeing you naked very much."

Her stare burns steadily into mine as she adds, "I meant what I said last night."

Whatever you do, I shall find pleasing, because you are mine.

I know I'm staring like a dumbass right now. But it had never occurred to me that someone could *like* messy people, that someone could find their embarrassments interesting or their revelations anything other than cringeworthy.

It's rather...freeing, actually. Like it doesn't matter if I do something wrong, if I get too needy or too clingy. It will all be delicious to her.

"So now," she says again. "Why is archaeology the only magic left in your life?"

I lower my hands, keeping my eyes on hers. Her gaze feels reassuring in its possession, as if she's used the ribbons on her arms to tie me tight to her, like she's already slipped a leash around my neck.

"I want things too much," I say simply. "So I had to stop. If not the wanting, then the wanting where everyone could see. It exhausted people, but it exhausted me too, you know? I hated feeling so needy, so gross, like some kind of vampire that couldn't quench her thirst no matter how much she drained from the world around her."

"You should never be less than yourself."

I sigh. It sounds like something a therapist would say, something that feels true inside a cozy, quiet room, only to ring hollow when you're hopelessly in love after only a single date or when you're making your friends wince because you're so sloppy at the club. When you're the person who wants to go out *again*, wants just one more drink, one more kiss, one more dizzy moment to sew up the night. It was why I kept burying myself in archaeology, despite the way it narrowed my world, because at least it would welcome my relentlessness, my restlessness. Another long night in the library? Another email pestering the grant coordinator about delivery of funds? Another several hours in the lab refitting pots? Archaeology would take it all, and it would never tell me I wanted too much from it.

So what if it killed the last of my fantasies, the last of my dreaminess? It had as much for me as I could ever wish for: a bottomless well of work to do and problems to solve.

"I don't say that as a platitude or a vacant reassurance, nor"—a smile tips the corner of her mouth—"would I say it to just anyone. Sholto, for example, would endear himself to me more if he were quite less himself. But for you, Janneth Carter, what does the world gain by you folding your hungers into the smallest possible square? When your hungers are so very lovely and have led you to dig into the earth for answers to questions most mortals have forgotten to ask?"

"I don't know," I say, a little absently. I think of the friends I've made in the past year or so, Alfie and François and a few others, friends whom I've been careful only to let see the most curated version of myself. Because even good people—even very cool, very smart good people—have their limits of patience, empathy, and good taste, and I'm done testing limits.

Or at least so I thought. Because here in Faerie, the limits seem as wide as the moors. Where else could I be a royal consort, eat a raw heart, fuck in the forest? Where else could I feel like I'm exactly the right amount and never too much?

"I've built a good life by folding myself into small squares," I say finally. "I'll graduate into a field that already has people waiting for me. I have friends who like me well enough."

"But who do not really know you," the queen points out. "Nor do you have lovers who know you longer than a night. Or even longer than a few hours, since you slip home before dawn."

My lips part. "I—I haven't told you any of that. How do you know?"

Her gaze is steady. "Do you want the truth?"

"Of course!"

"I've been watching you for a long time. Since you called for me."

"Called for you?" I echo. I literally have no idea what she's talking about.

Her hand finds my foot, and she strokes along the edge of its silk slipper. It's a firm enough touch to feel more possessive than ticklish, like she's petting me for her pleasure instead of my own. It makes me want to purr.

"Last Samhain, do you not remember?" she says, still with that idle stroking of my foot. "You called for me."

I think back to last year, sitting in my tiny flat in Edinburgh, loneliness heavy in my chest. Since my final year of undergrad, I'd been determinedly *easy*, and it had netted me all the results I'd hoped it would. I had a mentor who liked me in Dr. Siska, I had a few friends who weren't close but not too distant either. I had decent sex often enough to keep me from deleting my hookup apps.

But I'd been miserable, tired, uninspired. Nothing felt stirring anymore, nothing felt fun. And then I looked out my window and saw the torches moving through the narrow Old Town street.

I knew immediately I wanted to be down there. I shoved on shoes, grabbed a coat, and ran down to join the procession before I could change my mind. There were people painted woad blue and scarlet red, dancers dancing, singers singing, and all over shouting, chanting, drums, drums. The cold air felt crisp with a feeling I hadn't felt in so very long, and I'd closed my eyes in the crush of the crowd, one speck of grad student in the great scheme of nothing, and I surrendered myself one last time to the hope for magic. I begged magic to stay, to take me, to claim me, and when I opened my eyes to see the Summer King and Winter King facing off among fire and dancers and drums, I knew I wanted to be wherever that was real and not at all pretend.

I knew I'd offer up my heart whole for it to be real.

"Please," I whispered. I remember how the word was swallowed immediately by the drums. "Please take me. Take me and I'll go. I'll give you anything."

I hadn't been whispering it to anyone, had barely even whispered it to myself. The last gasp of a hope I had to smother and bury in the backyard of my mind so I wouldn't be haunted by it any longer.

"You heard *that*?" I ask now, still utterly confused.

Morgana nods, like of course, she heard a hushed plea over the clamor of drums and the trilling of half-naked neopagans. "Edinburgh may be at the very edge of the court's lands, but it's still my land. I hear every bargain offered by a mortal—which is a far smaller number than it used to be. Yours was the only bargain that intrigued me. So I watched you. I watched you through mirrors and puddles and the shine on the face of your watch and the glass of your phone. I watched you and I..." She pauses, looks down at my foot. Her hand now curls over the place where my metatarsals anchor to the rest of my foot. "I grew fascinated by you. I have wanted you for a very long time, Janneth."

A year. She's been watching me—wanting me—for a year. And while it's been a mortal year for me, it's been a Faerie year for her, at least twice as long. And then I remember the cairn, how Maynard knew my name when he found me, that they were *looking* for me.

For whatever opaque reason she has, it must be you. No one else.

Because she had been watching me. Because she'd chosen me, because I'd already made some kind of bargain with her without even knowing it. That's why I was taken. I'm not sure what to do with this information, because I should feel angry or scared or violated. I should not love that she watched me, chose me, took me for her own.

I shouldn't. I shouldn't.

"So this is why you kidnapped me," I say, trying to keep my voice neutral. Kidnapping is bad. I am wholesale, unambivalently against kidnapping and against being kidnapped.

Her hand holding my foot to her chair feels like home.

"Yes," she says simply. "This is why. I'm answering your bargain, Janneth. I took you, and now you're giving me what I want in return."

"Which is?"

"You," the queen says without inflection, like this should be obvious by now. She finds the hem of my dress and lifts it over my knees. She pushes my skirt to my hips in a pile of crystal and silk. And then she pushes my knees as far apart as they'll go, meaning my naked cunt is bared to her.

She touches the soft furrow of me, still sensitive from what we did in the forest, and then shamelessly presses against the tight ring below.

Kidnapping is bad. Magical stalking is bad. You didn't know you were making a bargain.

None of this is fair, and you should hate it.

I tilt my hips up, trying to chase her touch. She laughs at little at my unabashed need, but she does start toying with my clit, pushing her fingers into my mouth to get them wet and then rubbing the small bundle until I can barely think.

"Tell me what you're thinking," the queen murmurs. "Tell me something true."

"I'm thinking that I shouldn't love this so much," I breathe. "I'm thinking I should stop you, that I should try to get away." I shudder as she fits her fingers into the opening of my cunt, sinks inside. "I'm thinking I'm so fucking grateful that I was on your land that night and not the Thistle Court's."

Morgana's eyes flash, as if the mere idea of me being with another queen makes her furious. "You should be grateful," she says tightly. "The Thistle Court is dangerous."

"You're dangerous too."

She doesn't disagree. She can't because she cannot lie.

But she does bend her head down and nip at my inner thigh—hard and swift. "They killed my mother," she says. She's still working her fingers inside me as she says this, as if murder is totally normal sex talk. "Two years ago. They murdered her without provocation, without even the pretense of war. We are a Seelie court, they are Unseelie—perhaps that was reason enough, but I suppose what they craved was chaos. They knew the succession wasn't settled on either Morven or me, that my mother's untimely death without a chosen heir would create imbalance and strife. And they were right. The two years since I've claimed the crown have been like walking along the cutting edge of a knife. Sharp and joyless. Until you."

Until you.

My heart is a kite, beating around the inside of my chest.

She bends her head, still bound with her antler crown, and for the first time, I feel the hot velvet of her tongue between my legs.

She's unfairly good at this, knowing just how long to flick her tongue over my clit before replacing her fingers with it and fucking me that way. She knows when to suck and how hard, and she knows how to pump her fingers just right, matching the fullness inside to the work of her wicked mouth outside. The tines of her crown dig into the tender skin of my inner thighs.

I think...I think I'm in love. It's too soon and she kidnapped me and also she's terrifying sometimes and also I've spent half my time here blissed out on the nectar of her cunt—but also in the flicking candlelight, I see the marks her crown leaves on the inside of my thighs, I feel her mouth like sin itself curling against my flesh, and I think I'm in love.

She's cold and inhuman, and she kissed me in the forest with heart blood smearing her mouth, and I think I'm in love.

And when I think of her wanting me for the past year, of the way her voice goes low and smoky when she says things like *mine* and *until you*...

Well, I don't know if fairy queens love like mortals do. But even if it can't be love, the way she wants me is enough. It's more than enough. It's more than I ever knew I could hope for.

And so a little voice whispers, *You could stay*.

I could ask the queen to ignore her promise in the library and let me stay. Indefinitely. I could leave behind student loans and long nights in the lab and app-initiated one-night stands, and I could have an antler crown marking up my thighs, I could have fairy fruit, I could have her and an entire new world.

I could stay.

I come with a hot rush of pleasure, surging against her tongue, and she makes a disapproving noise when I move too much for her. She bands an arm over the top of my hips and holds me fast to the table while she fucks every last bit of my release out of my body. Fingers curling, mouth sucking, tongue like soft, soft fire.

And then, as the clenching waves recede and I can breathe again, she licks me clean and then sits up.

"Not as good as fairy fruit, I imagine," I joke weakly, and she shakes her head.

"It's better," she says, and she can only tell the truth, so who am I to argue?

She reaches up to brush some hair away from my face, and her mouth—still wet with me—parts, as if she's about to speak.

But she doesn't. She doesn't speak. She shakes her head instead, like she's silently chiding herself. "Let's get ready for bed," she says after a moment and pushes back her chair to stand. "Tomorrow brings the negotiations—and the Sanctuary—and some things are better faced with rest."

CHAPTER 14

When I wake, I'm in the queen's arms with my pulse racing and her thigh between my legs. I've just come, I think, in my sleep. I blink my eyes open to see her watching me with an amused expression.

"I would tell you *good morning*, but I believe you've made sure your morning is good regardless," she murmurs, and I press my lips to her collarbone.

"Let me lick your cunt before we go," I say, sleepily batting my eyelashes, and she laughs. I love her laugh, rich and dark as it is, and I love it all the more for the sense that it's a very rare thing.

"There will be time enough at the Sanctuary," she says, unwinding her arms from me and sitting up. Her dark hair tumbles around her shoulders and back, mussed and intimate.

I look at the visible slivers of her glassed back through her hair as I sit up too. "And what is the Sanctuary again?"

"It's a meeting place," she says. "Anchored by fae magic, bound by fae treaties. It's the one place by law where one cannot be attacked or killed."

"And we're doing your negotiations there?"

"We are," she says, swinging her legs and climbing easily out of her bed. Even though this is a pavilion and not a castle, her bed is still fit for a royal, massive and piled with silk and soft wool.

"Then how will there be time for sex?"

She's naked, and I admire the strong lines of her thighs, the taut curve of her backside as she searches out a robe. Her stomach is as flat as mine isn't, her breasts slight and pert, and I sigh unhappily as it all gets covered up with a robe. How, in a world where time stretches and bends, is there always so much to do?

"The Sanctuary—and the Shadow Market as a whole—is a very carnal place," Morgana says, belting the robe and finding a silver comb. "You will be there as my pet, and as my pet, it would be expected for you to attend to me the way a pet should. And you need to know this: the more obvious it is that you belong to me, the safer you will be."

I can be a pet all day, and as I proved to the queen the other night, I have no issue fucking in public. But...

"*Safer*? Is the market unsafe?"

"As I mentioned, the Sanctuary itself is bound by a treaty, so no harm comes to anyone there. But what happens there can have ramifications outside its boundaries...as well as after the Shadow Market closes tonight."

She explains a bit more as we dress to ride back to the castle. The Shadow Market is hosted by the fae—what the people of Faerie call themselves—every year, and it is a druid embodying the spirit of Cernunnos who lowers the veil between realms so the market is possible. And it is a different fae court's task to raise the veil again once the festival of Samhain is over. Last year the Court of Harps closed the market; next year it will be another, because Faerie is made of hundreds of courts, large and small. I suppose that's why something like the Sanctuary is necessary—a place outside the territorial wars and grudges all these courts seem to have with each other.

I'm also surprised to hear there are other realms besides my own and Faerie, but I'm not as surprised as I was two days ago when I learned fairies are real in the first place.

Never underestimate the human capacity for accepting weird shit, I guess.

"So what is the tithe?" I ask as our horses clatter up to the barbican.

The queen takes a minute to answer, and she doesn't look at me as she does. "That word is rarely spoken aloud and considered to be the greatest secret Faerie keeps. Where did you hear it?"

"When Maynard and Idalia took me," I say. "At the cairn. 'If the tithe fails, we will all pay the price.' Idalia said that."

We're coming through the barbican now and into the stone-and-grass courtyard. We bring our horses to a stop.

"It is a tax," Morgana says finally. "A price the fae pay to renew themselves. Every seven years. Seven years ago, it was the Thistle Court's turn to pay it. Now it is my own court's turn."

"It can't be that much of a secret. There are human stories about it," I say as we dismount and hand off our horses to the grooms. We will change into clothing worthy of the queen's diplomacy and then ride fresh horses to the market. "The tithe. 'At every seven years, they pay a tithe to Hell. And I'm so fair and full of flesh, I'm feared 'twill be myself.' That's from a poem about Tam Lin," I add.

"Yes, I know it," says the queen.

"It sounds kind of human sacrifice-y," I point out, looking at her. "Does that mean when the Thistle Court paid the tithe...?"

"The mortal stories are missing some key details," the queen replies. "And I should not be speaking of this to you as it is. We need to get ready for the market before we're late, anyway."

AN HOUR LATER, and we're back in the courtyard. Morgana wears a white gown without a back, its raw silk edges revealing the delicate glasswork of her body. It's the first time I've ever seen her wear something that exposes her glass, and I wonder if it's to impress whoever will be at the negotiations. Or maybe it's to show them she's unafraid.

She mounts her horse and then accepts a fur-lined cloak from a servant with hair made of thorny yellow gorse. As Morgana clasps it at her neck, Morven comes into the court-yard, dressed all in black and glowering at his sister.

"Don't do this," he says as he approaches her horse.

"To which *this* do you refer, Brother?" Morgana asks as she finishes fastening her cloak. "You sulk and fume about everything I've done for the past two years, so forgive me if I struggle to identify what's bothering you today."

His jaw is tight as he looks up at her. "You may wear the crown, but that doesn't save you from being a fool. You know she'll eat this entire kingdom whole if given a chance. And when it comes to tonight..."

He doesn't finish, but I guess he doesn't need to, because the queen gives a slow nod, as if she knows what he wants to say. She almost looks...sad.

"I have more laid in my lap than where I should melodra-matically prowl next, Morven," she says tiredly. "I need to go make sure the gifts are packed and ready. Janneth, stay with Idalia, and I'll rejoin you soon."

"You wanted this!" Morven calls as she rides out of the courtyard to the stables. "You fought me for it!"

But she, of course, doesn't answer.

He turns to me, his beautiful face a pale gold in the autumn sunlight. "Did she tell you whom she's meeting? Whom she's treating with?"

I shake my head silently.

"The Court of Thistles," he says. He is angry, cold, spitting the words. "The same fae who killed our mother. The same fae who war on us, prey on us, pluck at our borders and send assassins into our halls."

"Maybe she thinks a peace treaty will stop all that."

I think I detect something like pity in his obsidian eyes. "A peace treaty? Is that what you think this is? The Queen of the Thistle Court wants marriage, Janneth, and she won't settle for less. She wants to be wedded to my sister so the Thistle Court and the Stag Court will be reunited. Two queens, one court. A single crown of bone and thistle once again."

I stare at him, a strange, urgent tearing in my chest, like all the vessels around my heart are spilling blood all at once.

Morgana is getting married.

Morgana is getting married, and she didn't tell me.

Morgana is getting married, and now I am confronted with all the shameful, half-formed fantasies I've been harboring since I met her.

"Your precious queen is dragging you to her betrothal," Morven says. "Her betrothal to her mother's murderer. Not," he adds darkly, "that any of it will matter after tonight." He turns to leave.

"Wait, why won't it ma—"

But he's already striding away, fast and angry.

I look down at my hands, tight on my reins, and try to think. Try to reason past the pulpy, gashing hurt of it.

She's getting married.

It's one thing to be a pet, a consort, but a mistress? Do I think I'm made of stern enough stuff to watch Morgana sit next to someone else, converse with someone else, place trust in someone else?

Do I think I'm strong enough to watch her fall in love with someone else?

It could hardly be a love match, I try to reassure myself. *The Thistle Court literally just tried to kill her.*

But does it matter? When someone else would have first rights to her time, her bed, her thoughts? It might not be love, but it would mimic it, and it would kill me to watch.

I find Idalia by her cloud of moths, fluttering in the sunlight, and ride toward her, doing my best to look poised and cool and not on the verge of tears.

Not utterly humiliated.

But as we start on our ride to the market, all I can see is the queen's head bent between my thighs last night, her eyes right before she kissed me with blood on her mouth.

Her voice as she said, *I have wanted you for a very long time.*

WE CATCH up to Morgana and her small retinue, and she gestures for me to ride beside her. I fight the urge to ignore her, to storm off and ride back to the castle, because I don't want her to know how devastated I am. I don't want her to see the sprawling, grasping neediness I've allowed to bloom in just two days here.

Insatiable.

Insatiable enough to think I could have a queen of fairyland for my very own.

She seems preoccupied too, and I wonder if she's thinking of the Thistle Queen. Of her future bride. I wonder if this was why my bargain was amenable to begin with—a willing mortal pet for a few days, packed off in time to start planning a nuptial feast.

That's fine. It's fine. I'm leaving anyway, I'm going home tonight, and I *want* to go home tonight, and so it's all fine. Someday this will all be a joke to me. Remember that time I fell in love with a fairy queen, ha ha? Remember that time when I almost felt like I was exactly where I belonged? Hilarious. Now back to the student loan website that crashes every time I try to load it.

Everything in Faerie is larger, farther apart, but even so, I recognize the way we're taking to the market. We ride past a massive loch, up a twisting road to the crest of a hill, and then down to a fielded plain. Just to the west, there's a twisting grove of trees that leads all the way to the sea, cliffs of sheer stone pockmarked with caves, and the dun-gray teeth of some standing stones. There's even a castle.

From all other directions, fog creeps, fluttering like a veil in the wind, and in the middle of it all sits the market. A sprawling village of stalls, tents, pavilions, forges, kitchens, jousting lists, and stores that sell mortal wares like peanut butter and cell phone chargers and T-shirts that say *Eat the Rude*.

And it's *packed*. Packed like Walt Disney World in July. Packed like a grocery store before a snowstorm—or a pub on Tuesday nights when you can get half off drinks with your student ID. Crimson demons with black horns and claws, piratical centaurs, and foxes with many tails crowd the spaces between the stalls, jostling horned fae, tailed fae, courtly fae in magnificent dresses, and many others. As we dismount our horses and hand them off to Morgana's servants, I hear an unearthly wail and wonder if it's a banshee. We pass a bird-headed creature pulling a tank of water on a rickety wagon; a slender merperson waves from inside. There are people who don't have any nonhuman appendages or features but who are nonetheless dressed in clothes so strange that I think they must be magical too. Chitons and long black robes and armor that seems to shimmer and move even when the wearer is standing stock-still.

"How do mortals not notice this is here?" I wonder aloud. It's beyond noisy, with music, shouting, haggling, cheering, and it's a huge place. Already I feel lost, and we've only just begun wending our way through its alleys.

The queen doesn't answer, but Idalia does. "They see a glamoured version," she tells me as her moths bob around us. "Or rather, a special section of the market, just for them. A human carnival."

The carnival! No wonder it gave my fellow grad students weird vibes.

"So there aren't any mortals in this part of the market?"

"In theory, that's how it's supposed to work," Idalia says. "But some mortals come to trade or to buy. Others are lured in." She gives a toothy smile. "It's technically not supposed to happen, but the market is full of hungry folk..."

Something tells me she's not talking about french fries.

The Sanctuary is in the heart of the market, a tent the size of a circus big top, made of flapping white silk with foxgloves carpeting the space around it. I feel something charged and air-crackling—the wards enforcing the treaty, Idalia tells me—and then we're inside. Except it doesn't look like *inside*, it looks like a Highland glen: a high, rocky waterfall spilling into a pool and then a small burn, trees and ferns and fog. Birds and breeze and afternoon sunlight from...somewhere.

Fae and other folk mill about, some sitting, some standing, and I quickly note that it wouldn't take long for me to disappear in this fake wilderness.

I should try to leave now.

The thought comes quickly and then lingers, like the ring of a bell. This would be the perfect time, the perfect chance.

And why would I stay? To play the queen's pet while she plans a royal wedding? To service her needs while she plans her honeymoon with someone else?

I have a masochistic streak a mile wide, but even I have my limits.

I just wish it didn't *hurt* so much. I wish I hadn't fallen in love or hoped for—well, even now, I don't want to admit what I'd hoped for. The plan had always been for me to leave Faerie tonight anyway. The plan is unchanged.

No harm, no foul.

"You're upset," the queen says as we walk toward the waterfall. Idalia and the others in the retinue have fallen back, so I'm the only one who can hear her.

I want to be petulant as fuck and not answer her at all, but I also want *so badly* to be the kind of person who bears heartbreak stoically and with great dignity. "I'm not," I say, chasing that dignity so hard that I forget Felipe's advice. I've lied.

The queen stops, her eyes flashing. The retinue stops too, well enough behind us that there's at least the pretense of privacy.

"Do *not* lie to me," she says. "You've been upset since the castle, and I will discover why, although I cannot do it here. In the meantime, I will remind you that you need to play the part of pet now and play it well."

Well, now my pride is wounded on multiple fronts. "I've already proved I'm a great pet, haven't I?"

Her long lashes block most of the light from getting to her eyes, and they're like wells of night. "This is not a game, Janneth. I do not wish to be separated from you, and so I've brought you with me, but there are those in the market who will not hesitate to snatch you away once you're outside the Sanctuary, and the Court of Thistles will see you as a threat if they understand what you mean to me."

"And we wouldn't want your future bride knowing what I

mean to you," I put in, unable to resist, but I want to fling myself into the magical tent-river the minute I say it. It shows my hand too much. My neediness.

Those dark eyes soften. "Is that what this is about? Janneth—"

"Morgana, do you plan to keep me waiting all day?" comes a high, musical voice. I look over to see a woman with light-green skin, pink hair, and thorns growing from the ridges of her ears and along her cheekbones. She wears a pale green gown made of velvet, heavily boned and embroidered. "My time might be infinite, but your mortal pet's is not, so perhaps we should get started?"

CHAPTER 15

Morgana's shucked her cape, exposing the beautiful glass skin of her back as we follow the Thistle Court to a small clearing near the waterfall. She is glassed and there's Idalia's moths, and everyone else is tailed or furred or horned or thorned, and I feel very conspicuous.

Not simply because I'm the only mortal here, but because I garbed myself like a pet back at the castle, imagining myself purring at the queen's feet while she sliced some unwitting diplomat apart with her inscrutable eyes—but now I just feel cheap knowing I'm in front of her bride-to-be dressed like a slut. I'm wearing a gown of fluttery red chiffon, a strappy number made with some fairy clothing magic that holds it up even with a barely there bodice and no back to speak of. The dress sports a high slit and is thin enough that in the right light, you can make out the curves and dips of my body.

I'm very glad I grabbed my mortal coat at the castle to cover up with—not trusting some Tudor-esque cloak to do what good old-fashioned water-resistant polyester can. But then the Thistle Queen and the Queen of Stags sit on chairs carved to look like berry-laden brambles, and Idalia slips the coat from my shoulders, and I'm there in all my slutty glory. I take a deep breath to steady myself as the Thistle Court folks rake their eyes over me. I've been far sluttier in far more compromising positions, after all. I once spent twenty-four hours in Berlin wearing nothing but nipple pasties and a neon-green tutu.

The chairs the queens took are the only two chairs in the small clearing, each set at opposite ends of the space, so the queens will face each other when they sit. And when Idalia nudges me toward the queen, I understand I should sit at her feet. Both my pride and my sad, pulpy heart flail at this, but then I see the Thistle Queen watching me with eerie green eyes, and I remember the blood of her courtier spilling across the floor of Morgana's castle. Blood that was meant to be Morgana's.

The Court of Thistles will see you as a threat if they understand what you mean to me.

No, I can't test Morgana's patience here. If I succeed in provoking a reaction from her, they will see that I can affect her feelings. If she's lenient with me and allows some display of defiance, they could interpret that lenience as affection. Both are dangerous for me and for her, and so I don't fight Idalia when she nudges me again. I sit quietly at Morgana's feet and lean my head against her knee, the way I would have before I knew she was getting married. And I hate that it feels so right. I hate that I never want to move.

"I see why you like her," the Thistle Queen says, her voice carrying as she regards me with grasshopper-green eyes. "She's pretty."

Morgana drops a hand to curl into my hair. "Very pretty," she replies, her voice cool. Yet I hear the tautness in it. "But I'm not here for compliments, Acanthia. Tell me your terms and I'll decide if they're worthy of consideration."

The Thistle Queen tuts. "So direct, little doe." Morgana's

hand in my hair tenses the tiniest bit at the endearment. "But you are young," concedes Acanthia, "and you do not know how the game is played."

"If you'd like to blame my youth, you may," says Morgana, sounding very much as if she'd like to say more and is only barely holding herself back. For the first time since I've met her, I *feel* her youngness, her inexperience. She is uncertain here, in a way Acanthia is not. "You have offered marriage, and I am willing to listen to why I should accept it, but as you've noted, I have a very pretty pet to play with and would rather not spend the rest of my Samhain here."

There's no mistaking the irritation in Morgana's tone, and I'm relieved to see she is no more in love with the Thistle Queen than I am...but I'm also a little worried now. At her display of emotion, at how she's brought me back into the conversation unprovoked. I suddenly feel like more of a liability to her than her glassed back.

"You already know my terms, Morgana. I've made them plain enough in my letters. Let thistles crawl up the antlered throne, and reunite two courts that never should have been sundered in the first place. Let my child inherit and let their issue become the rulers of the Court of Thistles and Stags."

"I'm still unable to see the benefit in it for me. For my folk."

"Is peace not enough, Morgana? Knowing that if these talks fall through, you will have more war from us, and that eventually we will win?" A smile curls the Thistle Queen's pink mouth. "Or perhaps you are worried you won't have enough time for your mortal pet if you have a fae wife? But that won't be a problem after tonight, will it?"

Morgana's hand goes still in my hair, and even though I can't see her face, I'm certain she's angry. Or afraid?

But that can't be right.

"Besides, you'll find me as diverting as any mortal

consort." Acanthia looks at me again, dark green lashes dipping as she works her mouth to the side—an expression that would look coy on almost anyone else, but which on her looks dangerous. "But perhaps I underestimate this one. Maybe she should show me what it is about her that has you so interested?"

I can feel the tension coiling in Morgana's thigh and calf, like she's about to stand, and her hand has dropped from my hair to the back of my neck in a way that feels protective and possessive all at once.

And I see the trap Acanthia has laid here. I was right earlier: I am the liability, I am the weakness that can be exploited, and as hurt as I am by Morgana keeping this whole thing from me, I'm also not ready to be the reason she gets dicked over by her fairy rival. As stupid as it might be, she has my heart.

And if I'm leaving tonight anyway, maybe I can leave her a little better off than I found her—or not worse off diplomatically, at the very least.

I get to my knees. "I'd be happy to show you, Your Majesty," I say to the Thistle Queen. I glance up at Morgana so she can see that I want to do this, that I'm more than happy to. Morgana looks down at me, and I see the question in her inky eyes.

I see the warning.

I nod my head the tiniest bit. And quickly, before I can react, Morgana takes my jaw and delivers a kiss on my mouth —hot and open and velvet soft. I know right away what she's doing: she's making sure the first fairy fruit I taste today is from her. It's a claim on me and my body, a display of ownership for Acanthia's benefit. And maybe also for my own.

I don't care, I love it. And the minute the fruit hits my blood, I love it—and her—so much that I can barely breathe for it.

SIERRA SIMONE

"I do not want you to do this," she whispers against my mouth. "Only signal, and I will stop it. I will stop it all."

I press my hand to hers where it still curls hard against my jaw. "Let me."

She searches my gaze and then sighs. She releases my face. I stand and walk over to Acanthia before Morgana can change her mind, and then I sink to my knees.

"Your Majesty," I say, ducking my head, and she leans forward to lift my chin with one long thorn-knuckled finger.

"You don't need to be afraid of me," she says. "I cannot hurt you here."

Not incredibly reassuring, but I find I'm not that afraid anyway. Not with Morgana here. Her presence is as palpable and reassuring as a hill at my back. "Yes, Your Majesty."

Acanthia moves her hand to my hair and leans down to kiss me. I open my mouth obediently for her, allow her inside my mouth. I find her kiss floral and a little bitter too, but not in a bad way. More like fresh herbs, newly plucked, or maybe grass in the summer sun.

The fresh dose of fruit hits me hard, sending heat to the fast-slickening place between my legs.

The Thistle Queen doesn't kiss me long, but I didn't expect her to. This is about testing Morgana's patience and evaluating whether her feelings for me would make her stupid, and with the lusty fae, there seems to be one surefire way to do that. Acanthia pushes my head down, her intention clear. She hasn't raised her skirts for me, making me be the one to lift the heavy velvet enough to expose her need, and when I glance up to make sure I've pleased her, I find her staring at Morgana with an amused expression.

Her hand tightens in my hair, and I can't see anymore as she pushes my mouth to her cunt, but I'm certain she's still giving Morgana that same look. Daring Morgana to place her feelings for a temporary mortal pet over the future of her court.

Acanthia's sex smells of honeysuckle and fairy fruit, and at the first lick, I am tumbling headlong into ecstasy. I lap eagerly at her furrow, parting her to get to the slickness inside, and once I get there, a slow-rolling orgasm detonates just behind my clit, making me tremble and clutch Acanthia's pale green thighs to keep myself upright. I don't stop giving head, though, unable to stop, unable to bear not having just one more hit.

"I forgot how wonderful mortals are," Acanthia croons, not to me but to Morgana. "They thrill just to taste us, don't they?"

Even through the fruit haze, I feel a little smug to hear that her voice is unsteady at the end, a little breathless, because yeah, I'm pretty fucking good at this.

I push a finger into the queen's entrance, and then another. And then, with both hands in my hair, she pulls me tight to her and starts rocking against me. I give her the flat of my tongue to rub her clit against, and there's velvet spilling over my head, and I wonder if Morgana's watching, if she's jealous, if she wants to come over here and haul me off to use me like she did in the forest, riding my face until every breath smells like her.

The thought wrings another cataclysm out of me, and I whimper against Acanthia as she also tumbles over the edge, fast and quick. Her inner muscles move around my fingers, and I taste the fresh fruit of her release. And though she doesn't cry out or moan, her breath does hitch. Her body curls over mine the slightest bit.

When I pull back to look at her over the tumble of her velvet skirts, she looks a little stunned. And now I'm a *lot* smug. I mean, mostly horny and stoned, but smug too.

But she recovers quickly, pulling me up for a long kiss, which she trails to my jaw and to my ear.

"Little pet, you are quite something," she murmurs. "I can see why she adores you. Not so much that she won't pay the tithe, but it will hurt her to do it, be sure of that."

I turn my head, and I don't know if it's to look at her or to taste her mouth again. "The tithe?" I ask, a little confused. "Hurt?" All I can think of is Tam Lin, of the little rhyme-y words. They dance in my fruit-soaked thoughts.

At every seven years, they pay a tithe to Hell.

And I'm so fair and full of flesh, I'm feared 'twill be myself.

"Oh, I thought you knew," she says, voice hushed and full of sweet concern. "It's up to the Court of Stags to pay it this time. Up to Morgana."

The queen had said as much before we came here, but I must have missed the part where it would *hurt* her to pay the tithe.

If it's a tax, then can't taxes wait? Is there a fairy IRS she can complain to about this?

I want another kiss. I want to dive under Acanthia's skirts again. Magic swirls in the air, pulses through me. But the magic pulls at my thoughts too, pulling them down to the earth beneath my knees, pulling them down to this very moment.

Think, a voice in my mind whispers. *Ask*.

"Can't she just not...pay it this time?" I ask dazedly.

Acanthia laughs. It reminds me of wind on the hills, of days that look like they should be warm but are somehow cold as shit instead. "The tithe is what holds our entire world together," she tells me, still too low for anyone but me to hear. "If the tithe isn't paid, then Faerie unravels. And then all the realms that use fae magic to tether them together unravel too. If the tithe isn't paid, the veil stays open, and it will be as it once was in times of old. Death, famine, war between all the realms, all within a year. Maybe sooner."

I want to protest, I want to tell her that can't be true, that all these worlds can't just fall apart because of some unpaid fee...but Acanthia can't lie. About anything.

"And you know how we pay the tithe, right?" She kisses my cheek, my jaw again. My neck. Her kisses feel so good, everything feels so good, even as my mind struggles against the fruit to think. Morgana watches us, her eyes dark, her shoulders tense, like she's keeping herself from leaning forward to hear us, since Acanthia is speaking for my ears alone.

"I don't know," I mumble, my eyes fluttering at the pleasure of her mouth behind my ear.

"With the life of beloved things. Beloved *ones*. Consorts, lovers, kings and queens. Pets."

When beloved things bleed, the land sings.

My eyes open. "What?"

She pulls back enough that I can see her eyes glittering like emeralds. "That's right, little one. You're to be the tithe tonight."

Fear somehow finds its way into my blood, washed away quickly by the haze of the fruit, but its metallic tang lingers in my mouth. "No," I say, turning to look at Morgana. "She promised I could leave Faerie."

I see Morgana sitting across the little glen from us, her full mouth set in a regal, distant line. I know her well enough now to know that cool mask hides quite a bit, and sure enough, her chest is moving quickly with some deep feeling. Her obsidian eyes flash as they meet my gaze, and for a moment, I'm struck by how painfully beautiful she is. Those high cheekbones, those perfectly arched brows. The long neck and delicate clavicle and those slender but wicked hands.

"She promised," I say again. "And she can't lie."

"Of course she can't," Acanthia soothes in my ear. "But

think, pet—what did she actually promise you? Was it to let you leave? Or did she only make you think so?"

You shall be my pet, my everything, until the final night of Samhain, and you will not be harmed until you leave Faerie.

Leave Faerie—that had felt so unequivocal to me. I'd get to go home, right? Unless...unless leaving Faerie hadn't meant going home at all. Unless leaving Faerie meant *dying*.

I let out a shaky breath. She'd been right the night of the feast. She'd tried to warn me herself. There are many, many ways to lie.

And she'd lied about this without having to do any work at all; I'd practically handed it to her with my own assumptions.

"You see now," Acanthia says softly. "You are the obvious choice for the tithe. The alternative is chaos and madness for every fae, demigod, or creature in the realms. You mustn't blame her, though," she says sensibly. "It is the way things are and always have been. And I do promise you that it will hurt her. She will hate every moment of killing you."

This is my consort, a mortal worthy of a stag's heart and a stag's kiss. So too shall she be worthy of a stag's fate.

I think of Morgana's hands on the crossbow, of the thick wooden bolt sinking into the stag's chest. Of how we ate its raw heart, blood dripping down our chins.

A stag's fate.

I swallow, staring across the glen at the queen I fell in love with, at the queen I trusted. The fruit is making me dizzy, making my hurt blurry, my fear fleeting.

"But you could leave before the tithe is due," Acanthia says thoughtfully, as if this has just now occurred to her. "You could go back to your mortal lands before midnight and get far away from her before she can pay the debt."

"What happens then?" I ask. We're quiet enough that I know Morgana can't hear, but the longer we speak, the more and more displeased she looks. "Will someone else have to be the tithe?"

"Perhaps, but perhaps not—the tithe must be beloved of the ruler, and how many do you think in the Court of Stags are beloved of the crown? Morgana's courtiers? Her dour little Spaniard? The brother who curses her every footfall? Doubtful. So maybe she will not find someone else."

"But then the tithe will fail," I say slowly. "Isn't that also a problem?"

"But you will be *alive*," Acanthia says. "That's what matters." And then she adds, "This is not your problem to solve, Janneth. You were chosen for this without your knowledge; you were brought here against your will. You have no duty to Faerie or its woes. Flee and live, and let Faerie pay for its own sins for once."

"But how can I leave?" I ask. "Without her noticing?"

"Oh, little pet," Acanthia says quietly, with a quick kiss to my head. "Let me worry about that. Take your chance when you see it—and don't stop running until you reach the Castle Docherty. There's a doorway to the mortal world there."

She stands up behind me, and I feel her skirts fall to the grass as she does. She steps around me toward Morgana with her hand outstretched.

"You have excellent taste in pets, Morgana," she says loudly. "And I'm well pleased with your gift of her. But we must, as you intimated earlier, focus on the matter at hand. Take a turn with me, away from the ears of our courts, and allow me to make my case one last time."

Morgana looks at me. "She needs salt."

Salt. My mind drifts to my ugly polyester coat. To its pocket.

"She'll be fine," Acanthia croons. "Won't you, pet?"

This is the play. Acanthia will lead Morgana off, and I'll run the minute I can. I will run home, and it won't matter that I'm running away from the one person who's chosen me, who's wanted me, because that person is also probably going to kill me for a magical fairy tax, according to someone who literally can't lie about these things.

And maybe I'm in love with Morgana, but I've also watched her torture a servant and eat a heart raw. I've also heard about how she magic-stalked me for a year.

I'm not sticking around to find out exactly how safe I am.

"Yes," I say softly, ducking my eyes so I don't have to see Morgana's cold beauty as I speak. The fairy fruit is still pounding in my blood, swirling in my gut, demanding more, demanding pleasure, hedonism, sex. *Good*. I want them to think I'm drunk, stoned, too dazed to escape. That I'll stay exactly where I'm left, bound by the need for more fruit. "I'll be fine."

Morgana's lips press briefly together; she lifts her chin. "I won't be long," she tells me, as if she still has the right to make me feel safe. "I'll be right back."

And then she stands, refusing Acanthia's hand but walking with her toward the waterfall all the same. Most of the courtiers, including Idalia, follow, keeping a respectful distance from the monarchs and seeming to forget about my very existence. Because why would they care about a mortal panting after more fairy fruit? How much trouble could I possibly make?

Coat, my mind whispers. *The coat.*

I stand slowly and then creep to where Idalia draped my coat over a log. And then, with a few short steps, I'm around a grove of trees, walking quickly toward the exit of the sanctuary. My body burns against the cool air as I do, keening for more fairy fruit, the same way my heart keens for Morgana.

Salt, I remind myself. I need salt to break the spell. I reach for the little cutlery set in my coat pocket, the paper packet with a disposable bamboo knife and fork. I pull it out of my coat pocket as I walk out of the Sanctuary and tear it open.

Sure enough, at the very bottom are two tiny packets— one is pepper. The other is salt.

It only takes the first few grains for my mind to clear and my body to cool. And once it does, I slip on my coat, hike up my skirts, and run.

CHAPTER 16

The market is too crowded, too busy, and I have no idea where Castle Docherty is, but I shove my way through the fray regardless, my head down and the hood of my coat up over my blonde hair. Not that it helps any —in a place of horns, headdresses, and hair in every hue, my plain polyester hood is as much of a giveaway as anything else.

Castle Docherty. Castle Docherty.

It sounds familiar—one of the castles Dr. Siska investigated when she was looking for the site of de Segovia's castle, I think. Fourteenth century, with an outer fortress wall. Sandstone, maybe.

I scan above the stalls as I walk, looking for battlements and conical roofs emerging against the slow-fading sky. There's no way a castle can *hide*, not among tents and wide-open jousting lists, but it still takes me a good fifteen minutes of shoving my way through the crowd to see it at the very edge of the market, hulking in the twilight. Fog swirls at its base, and the weathered stone looks...worm-eaten somehow.

I can't say I particularly want to go there, because it looks haunted as fuck, but I'm also a little low on choices right now.

I squeeze through the crush—vendors calling out bargains and sales, buyers desperate to get what they need before the market closes—and finally see a grassy path between two pavilions that will take me to the castle. It looks very untrod and bedecked with spiderwebs, like no one else has wanted to go to the castle either, and maybe it's not a good idea to go off on my own—

A hand seizes my upper arm, yanking me back before I can get to the path. Choking back a yell, I spin and twist, trying to get away, but my assailant holds fast, their fingers digging into my arm through my coat. When I twist all the way around, I don't see the queen or one of her guards, or even a random fairy looking to prey on a lost-looking mortal. I see Felipe.

Felipe, whom I thought was a friend.

He shoves a cloth to my face, and no matter how I wrench and struggle, I can't seem to escape it. It smells earthy, faintly sweet, and then my muscles loosen. Darkness creeps at the edges of my vision, swirls in front of me.

"I'm sorry," he says in Latin. "I'm sorry for this."

I'M COLD.

I'm cold, and everything smells like wet stone and dirt.

I drag my eyelids open to see that I'm somewhere dim and enclosed, and at the same time, I become aware of the stone underneath me, of the cold metal binding my wrists and ankles. I'm cuffed and spread-eagled on some kind of slab, and the only light comes from a single blue-burning torch in the corner of the space.

Felipe stands underneath it, his clothes blending into the dark stone behind him, and his sad features disappear and reappear as the torch dances in the strange arrhythmic gusts of this presumably underground space.

"You're awake," he says softly. "Good."

"Where am I?" I rasp. I try to move, but the cuffs and chains are too heavy, and I'm still fucked up from whatever he dosed me with. "Back at the castle?"

He inclines his head. "You will be taken to the tithing place soon. But it is best if you are here until then."

I close my eyes, the fear colder than the metal anchoring me to the stone. "So it's all true. She's going to kill me tonight."

"It's a very old tradition," he says gently. "One that's stabilized the realms for as long as anyone can remember. She has no choice. Even the Thistle Queen did her duty—it's what real rulers must do."

And Morgana would be aware of that, sensitive to that. *Struggling*, Felipe had said of her at the hunt. *Young*, Acanthia had called her. The tithe would be a show of strength, proof she has what it takes to rule in this vicious world.

"So that's it," I say, so tired now. "I'm going to be human sacrificed. Wonderful."

And all because I hadn't wanted to bother Dr. Siska about lights around the excavation site when she was enjoying her evening tipple.

"I encountered a rumor once," he says quietly, "in a fae record from Devonshire. That the people there had once paid the tithe another way. That a life *paid* didn't have to mean a life *killed*. That you could sacrifice a life without ending it. But it was written like a riddle, and while I'd hoped I would untangle it before the Court of Stags had to pay the tithe again, I never could. And here we are."

I want to cry. I'm about to be *murdered* and he's talking about riddles. "Why did you drag me back?" I whisper, tears burning at my eyelids. "You're mortal too."

"Not truly," he says. "Not anymore. I have no mortal salt left in my blood, Janneth. If I go back, all the long years spent here will turn me into dust the moment I cross over. I can't ever leave...and so I must make sure I can stay. I must make sure I'm in the queen's favor, that Faerie stays safe and stable. You are the price for that."

He steps forward and touches my bare foot with his hand. My slippers are gone and so is my coat, and I'm just in that skimpy red thing, the chiffon skirt falling up to reveal my thigh, my tits spilling out of the tiny bodice. But there's nothing sexual in Felipe's touch. It seems more like an apology.

"Forgive me for not being there to watch tonight," he says. "Trust me, I take no pleasure in any of this."

And then his touch leaves my foot; his shadow moves. He leaves me alone, chained to a stone and waiting to die.

IT's so dark down here, and fairy time is so meaningless that I have no idea how much time passes between Felipe leaving and fresh footsteps coming down the corridor. A candelabra appears in the rough stone arch that marks the entrance of my cell, and I close my eyes against the bright glare.

I try to swallow back the panic. I try to tell myself that it's better to act calm now so maybe they'll lower their guard and I can escape. I tell myself that if I can't escape, then I at least want to die with some shred of dignity left.

But it doesn't matter. They're here to drag me off to my killing place, and the tears are burning hot tracks down my temples and into my hair, and I can't breathe, and I'm terrified. I'm so, so, so fucking terrified.

SIERRA SIMONE

The candelabra lowers, and I hear the whisper of silk on stone. "Janneth," Morgana says. "Please don't be frightened."

She's alone, but it doesn't matter. She probably has some special fairy-queen magic that would make it so she could drag me to my death without much effort at all. Hell, all she has to do is kiss me, and it would be that much harder for me to resist following her wherever she wanted me to go. Maybe that would be a blessing. Maybe wrapped in orgasmic ecstasy would be the best way to go.

The queen sets the light on the far edge of the slab and then strokes my hair, fingering the tresses like she's already forgotten how it feels between her fingertips.

"You are," she says, and there's a hitch in her breath when she speaks, "so very beguiling like this."

"Trapped?" I ask. "About to die?"

She doesn't reply, but her eyes answer enough for her. They linger over the cuffs on my ankles and wrists, on my nearly exposed breasts, with their tips taut from the cold. On where the skirt parts enough to show my thigh, where it could be parted farther to reveal my naked pussy.

She climbs up onto the slab with me, crawling over my supine form, and the white silk of her gown gapes at the bodice. I can see right down her dress like this. I can see her breasts, the perfect handfuls of them, the rosy nipples as hard as mine. I can see the line of her stomach and the well of her navel. There is a torc of antler bone around her neck, its points resting against her collarbone, and I wonder if it would dig into my skin if she kissed me. If it would leave marks all over me if she kissed her way down my body.

Despite everything, I respond to her. My heart is kicking. My belly is tight. I'll be wet very soon.

"Oh, Janneth," she murmurs, her fingers pulling at the chiffon covering my breasts, moving it to the sides so she can look at my nipples. They jut up, tight with cold but also ready for attention, and then, like that's not enough for her, she sits back and pushes the skirt of my dress apart so she can see my cunt too. She presses her thumbs to my labia and parts me, a satisfied noise leaving her at what she sees.

I'm twisting on the slab now, but to my great shame, it's not because I want to get away. It's because I want her to keep touching me, keep looking at me.

Because I want her to keep me, period.

"I could spend years just looking at you," she says in a murmur, echoing the squirming hopes of my stupid heart. Her gaze rakes from my spread cunt to my bared tits to where my head rolls on the stone. "Years and years. You look so beautiful right now. Let me feel you too, Janneth. I must feel you now." She says this last part as she slides her fingers deep into my core. I arch off the stone, and she leans forward, bracing her free hand by my head.

"You're so soft," she says. "And so sweet. Doesn't that feel good, pet? Doesn't that feel exactly like what you need?"

I shouldn't answer. She doesn't deserve an answer. But the answer is pulled from lips anyway. "Yes," I whisper. "Yes, it feels good."

She likes that, I can tell. Something like a smile curves her mouth as she drops her forehead to mine, truly fucking me now with long, delicious strokes, moving up with wet fingers to play with my clitoris. I pant underneath her, everything so tight in my stomach and thighs and chest, and here's the truth that I have to live with for the rest of my very short life: I never needed fairy fruit to become trash for Morgana. Even stone-cold sober—even knowing she's about to kill me—her amused little smile is enough to drag me to the edge. Her hand between my legs is enough to steal my breath, to drive all thought and reason from my mind.

Pleasure spikes through me, sharp thrills up my belly and

into my chest, and I can't move, I can't do anything but arch and whimper and wish she would kiss me.

She doesn't. Even as she fucks me, even as she gives me hard, slick strokes, she does nothing more than press her forehead to mine. Her mouth is *so close*, close enough that I could catch it, and I try, I try to find her lips, but every time I do, she moves back. Not much, but enough that I can't reach her.

I feel her breath against my lips. Her nose bumps into mine.

"Kiss me," I plead, but she doesn't, at least not in the way I want. She kisses my cheeks, my nose, my jaw. She gives me wet, biting kisses along my neck and my collarbone. She moves down to pull my nipples into her mouth, all searing velvet and pain-bright teeth, and then she moves so she can lower her head between my thighs.

I was right. I can feel her antler torc dragging and digging into me as she moves.

At the first hot stripe of her tongue, I cry out to the low stone ceiling, and at the second, I'm a wild thing in my chains. Trying to get more, trying to get away from the intensity of her kiss, I'm not sure, but it hardly matters, because I *can't* get away, I'm chained and spread for her, a sacrifice before the sacrifice to come.

Her tongue, wicked and clever, works me from side to side, over and over, fast enough to have me groaning, then slow, torturing, wringing whimper after desperate whimper from my lips.

The orgasm is a heavy thing, like another length of silver chain anchoring me to the stone, and it almost hurts as it ripples free, yanking and weighted in its pleasure. Morgana moves back up, a hand once again braced by my head, and while I'm still in the throes of my first climax, she uses the hand still between my legs to pull yet another out of me. Her touch is fast, hard. Inescapable. I don't even know what noises

I'm making. All I know is that I want her to kiss me, kiss me with that mouth still wet from me, and I don't even want the fairy fruit, because it's her I want. Just her. No fruit, no crown, nothing save for obsidian eyes and perfect aim and a flair for cruel pleasure—just her. Morgana.

I come again, of course, inevitable as it is, and the pleasure rolls in burning pulses up to my chest and down my thighs, and my scalp is tingling and so are the soles of my feet, and everything is breathless, dizzy, wonderful.

Except she still keeps her mouth away from mine.

"Kiss me," I beg. "Kiss me before you kill me."

She doesn't answer. She keeps her hand pressed against my swollen pussy, and her forehead to mine, and I can feel how heavy and hard her breaths are coming right now, like it's taking everything she has to stay still, to stay exactly how she is.

A long sigh shudders out of her, and she lifts her hand from between my legs and presses her wet fingers to my mouth. I kiss them, lick them, tasting myself, and then she drops her lips to her hand too. We're kissing, but with her hand between our lips.

Though she's so very close, I still see the moment her eyes close. A tear, hot and fast, drops from her lashes onto my cheek and rolls into my hair.

"Go," she says shakily. "Go, Janneth."

"Wait, what—"

She's already moving off me, swiping impatiently at her face as she unlocks the cuffs at my wrists and ankles with a mere press of her thumb. They click open, and once they're all unlocked, I scramble to the side of the slab and then to the ground, looking at her across the surface of the stone.

"Go," she repeats. "Take the torch and follow the hallway until you see a door carved with the sign of a rose. It will lead you out into the garden. From there, a trail will take you through to woods to the loch. The tomb will take you home."

I can't stop staring at her. The dark hair swept up and pinned with delicate carved bone, the glittering eyes. The high cheeks dusted with a flush that nearly looks gentian in the blue light of the torch.

The lips swollen from kissing me, but not on the mouth.

"You're saying I can just go," I say. My voice isn't inflected in a question or pitched as an assertion. It sounds as numb as I feel. "After all this...you're just going to let me go."

"Yes," she says, lifting her chin. "But you must hurry. It is close to midnight, and the witnesses will be gathering at the tithing place. They will be expecting you."

I'm still too shocked to move. "But what will happen to Faerie if the tithe isn't paid? What will happen to you?"

She meets my gaze. "I do not know for sure. But I do know that nothing means anything to me if you are not in the world, Janneth. I love you. Despite how stupid and foolish it makes me. Now go."

I want to tell her I love her too. I want to tell her that this love makes me stupid and foolish too, because even now the idea of leaving her feels akin to ripping out my own throat, and I want to tell her that all I want, even now, is to stay her pet forever, sitting beside her in fairyland.

I don't tell her these things.

I take the torch from the wall, glance back at her standing motionless in the room, candlelight making her a statue of gold and shadow, and then I do what she told me to do.

I go.

Chapter 17

The way out is as Morgana said: a rose-carved door, a garden, a narrow path through the woods. Thunder echoes through the trees as I hurry down the path as fast as I can; a low, angry storm is churning in from the sea. Lightning dances in the cloud bellies above me, and there's no rain yet, although I know it's just a matter of time before it reaches me.

My feet are bare, and I'm still in my chiffon dress, and I'm sure my tits are frozen off by the time I see the loch glinting through the trunks of the trees. I turn to look back at the castle, lit blue and gold against the night, and my heart twists like an apple being yanked from a branch.

I love you, I think. *No matter what you planned to do. I love you.*

And then I turn and start half jogging along the shore of the loch, relieved when I see the tomb's hulking shape. It's ringed with torches, just like it was in the mortal realm on the first night of Samhain, but there's no one there that I can see, no Maynard or Idalia waiting to kidnap me again, no Felipe ready to drag me back to the castle.

Elphame will just have to suffer. Unravel.

You have no duty to Faerie or its woes. Flee and live, and let Faerie pay for its own sins for once.

My steps slow.

I'm so close. I'm bedraggled and heartbroken and terrified, but I'm so close, and all I have to do is walk through the tomb, and I'm not walking through, I'm not coming any closer. I'm just standing in front of the cairn's open mouth like a statue, wishing it didn't matter to me that Morgana and her kingdom might suffer if the tithe isn't paid.

Morgana was going to kill you. She watched you for a year, adored you, craved you, knowing all the while she'd pay the tithe with your blood.

But I still can't make myself walk through the door.

Before I can decide what to do, a shadow moves in the tomb. I take a hurried step backward as the shadow resolves itself into the slender, muscular form of Morven Nightglass.

"I was hoping I'd be in time to see you off," he says. His posture is studied, casual, but he looks more rumpled than I've ever seen him, his platinum hair mussed and his shirt open all the way to the breastbone. He almost looks like he came straight from someone's bed, but when he steps closer and I see how hard he's breathing, how he still has a short cape clutched in one hand like he tore it off, I wonder if he's like this because he *ran* here.

To grab me and haul me back to the castle? Or worse, to the tithing place?

Panic claws up my throat, and my worry for Morgana and the fate of Faerie wavers under a cloud of cold fear.

"Are you here to stop me from leaving?" I ask, more to buy myself some time than anything else.

"Why would I, when it serves my purposes so well?" he says, again with a convincingly indifferent air. But there's no way he tore down here just to wave me off.

"Those purposes being what? Me being gone?" I ask, discreetly casting my gaze around the shore of the loch. I think we really are alone down here, and I think I might be able to get enough of a head start that I have a chance to make it *somewhere*...but where? Past him and into the tomb, where safety and home beckon? Or back up to the castle to try to help Morgana?

"How small you think," Morven says. "What of the crown my sister wears that I want so very much? What of a throne that could be empty at a moment's notice?"

I stop looking around; he has my full attention now. "The throne isn't going to be empty," I say. "Morgana will remain the queen, no matter what happens tonight."

His eyebrows lifted. "Is that so, little mortal? Even if she sacrifices herself for the tithe?"

In the hellish blur of the last few hours, it never even occurred to me that she might...no. No way.

"You're wrong," I say. Firmly. "Acanthia said it had to be someone beloved of the crown."

Morven looks at me like I'm stupid. "A Faerie crown is not a mortal crown, a metaphor for its wearer. It's an extension of the fae realm and the magic that binds it. And what's more beloved to Faerie than a Faerie ruler, Janneth? Than one whose blood and bones are tied with the land? Who can shift the mist and move the hills? Morgana's death would be powerful magic—the kind of magic our world was built on."

And then he sighs. "And unfortunately, my sister is far less ruthless than she should be when it comes to these things. Our court has Unseelie roots, and she would be better served by embracing them, by doing what Queen Acanthia would do and sacrificing you despite her obsession. But Morgana is too *noble* for all that. She believes a queen shouldn't ask anything of someone she is unwilling to do herself."

"Even death," I say faintly.

He nods.

"But you're wrong," I say again, a little desperately this time. "She would have said—if she was planning to pay the tithe with *herself*—no. She wouldn't do that."

She wouldn't send me away knowing she was going to take my place instead. She wouldn't have touched me, freed me, stared at me with those deep, inky eyes while I walked away and left her to die...

"This can't happen," I whisper. "It *can't*."

"She could, perhaps, offer the usual closing sacrifice rather than a tithe, using the same magic that's used to lower the veil in the first place. On non-tithe years, this is sufficient, and maybe it will close the veil enough to buy everyone some time."

"Yes," I say, grabbing on to this idea. "And if it works, maybe the tithe never needs to be paid again!"

"Or," Morven says, and he almost sounds gentle now, "it does not work. The veils stays open, and people like Queen Acanthia will once again be able to steal away mortal children, and the Court of Salt will be able to sink ships and eat their drowned sailors. Gods and demigods will roam the earth, demanding worship and glory. Witches will have no limits on their magic. It will be as it was in the past, in the times of tales, with monsters, mayhem, death. And that is only the beginning, because if the tithe is not paid to renew the land and the land begins to fail, the Salt fae and vainglorious demigods will be the least of anyone's problems."

I stare at him. "What?" *Mortal children...demigods roaming the earth...* "Acanthia didn't say anything about..."

"About the mortal world? No, I don't think she would, given that she'd like nothing more than for the veil to stay open so she can pillage it as she pleases. But yes—the tithe, the veil—all the magic that links and unlinks our worlds will be undone. And it won't just be fae who can creep among the mortals at will but demons and monsters too. Some will be good, if curious. Some will not."

I push my hands against my closed eyes, trying to breathe, trying to think. The stakes have just gone from helping Morgana to saving my entire world. I feel very fundamentally not cut out for this.

"And Morgana knows all this," Morven continues. "And so her choices were these: to kill her mortal lover, kill herself, or refuse to pay the tithe altogether. She could not stomach the first, and the last would potentially leave the blood of billions on her hands. I know you've not known my sister long, but between these choices, which do you think she would choose?"

I'm still numb, my mind as frozen as my body. I look at him. "Swear to me this isn't a trick. That this isn't a way to lure me back to the castle or the tithing place to kill me."

His eyes are as black as the storm above us when he meets my gaze. "I swear to you, Janneth Carter, that I speak the truth. My sister will try to pay the tithe with herself tonight; I believe you are the only one who can convince her otherwise. I cannot promise your safety if you go to the tithing place to stop her, but I *can* promise it is not my intention, aim, or hope that you will come to harm there yourself."

I mentally sift through his words as best as I can. I think he is telling the truth. I think it might also not matter even if he isn't. Because I can't risk Morgana dying.

I can't.

"Are you admitting you're doing this to help your sister?" I ask, taking a step forward. Closer, I can see the beginning of his glassed chest, the pink, red, and russet parts of him peeking from the open collar of his shirt.

He gives me a sour look. "Yes. But if you tell anyone else

that I wanted to help her, I will do everything in my power to make you look like a fool."

"Fine," I say. When he offers me his cape to drape over my shoulders, I take it and knot it tight at the neck. "Take me to her."

Come what may.

CHAPTER 18

The tithing place is near the market, deep in an ancient grove of trees by the sea. Morven doesn't take us there by any marked roads or paths—instead, we creep through the moss-carpeted trees and clamber up boulders, my torch doused and Morven's better eyesight guiding us.

My feet hurt *so much*.

"Why can't we just take the easy way through the market?" I ask in a low voice. The woods seem empty save for the thunder and creeping mist, but I don't know how close we are to the stones yet, and I don't want to risk being overheard.

"It's the tithe. It's secret," Morven says, as if that explains everything, but when I make an exasperated noise, he sighs.

"Most creatures, including the fae, believe the rituals used to lower and raise the veil are vestiges of our old worships, carried forward purely for the reason of hosting the market. And they are partly right—the market is a vital thing, and if that were the only reason for continuing our ancient rites, we would still do them. But those tasked with running a court of Faerie—a ruler and their closest advisors, Seelie and Unseelie alike—are given the truth. That death renews life, and that this renewal is due every seven years. And that's just here, in this part of Faerie. There are other parts of Faerie where tithes are demanded too."

I recall Felipe's mention of a tome from Devonshire. *The people there had once paid the tithe another way...*

"The rites used to lower the veil and then close the veil on a non-tithe year are an echo of the old magic. But the tithe *is* the old magic, the original magic. And it's so old and so secret that even our own people only hear rumors of it. Because it is an awful thing. Necessary, maybe, but awful. And so, on tithing night, it's hardly something we advertise by prancing through the market in full panoply. Fae rulers dislike speaking of it even with each other; it's that much of a taboo to acknowledge it aloud."

And yet the Queen of the Thistle Court had spoken of it quite readily to me in the Sanctuary. "I think Acanthia wanted this," I say, the truth of it feeling clearer and clearer as I speak. "I thought she was helping me escape just to upset Morgana, but I think she knew that if I left, Morgana would take my place, and no one else."

"That sounds like her," Morven says. "I suppose they think they'd have an easier time coaxing me into marriage...or war, after Morgana died and I took the crown. And they might be right. I'd make a terrible king."

He doesn't sound upset when he says it, nor does he seem like he wants a response. So I don't give him one, focusing instead on following him and keeping my bare feet mostly intact.

The lightning flickers constantly as we finally reach the place where the grove thins into a clearing, revealing the standing stones in their silent, crooked glory, ringed with blue will-o'-the-wisp torches. Morven gestures for me to stop well before we'd be in sight of anyone inside the standing stones, but it wouldn't matter anyway. Everyone in the circle is very, very preoccupied with themselves. Preoccupied with Morgana, who stands in the middle wearing nothing but her white silk gown and her antler-bone torc.

Her dark hair is unbound, hanging in soft waves down her back, but the breeze lifts and pulls at her hair, revealing over and over the exposed glass of her back. She is arguing, I think, with Sholto, who looks wildly upset, and Idalia, whose moths flit around in darting, panicked movements.

There is one other person here, dressed in simple clothes of white and green, with a leek pinned to their chest. They have long hair and a slender frame, and they stand with their hands laced in front of them. Morven tells me they are named Ynyr and that they come from the Court of Harps some ways south of here. Every Tithe must have a witness from another court, Morven says, and Ynyr has come to ensure the Stag Court pays their due. From the warm way Morven speaks of the Court of Harps, I sense they're not assholes like the Thistle Court.

"There is no other way, unless you are offering to volunteer," Morgana's voice carries over the wind. The trees around us creak like a boat in a storm. "It must be me. I choose for it to be me."

"So you will pay with your own life?" Idalia asks, her voice breaking. She's crying, and I don't think I'd considered before now that Morgana being *beloved* meant something more than the land being attached to her. Idalia is agonized right now. "You will end yourself because Acanthia wanted you to suffer?"

Pay. *Pay.*

I think again of Felipe and his riddle.

A life paid didn't have to mean a life killed.

"Morven," I ask quietly. "Is there a way to pay a life without that person dying?"

He looks at me, a line of confusion between his straight brows. "You mean, like dying and being reborn? Like a god?"

"I don't know, maybe?" I reply. "'Sacrifice a life without ending it,' that's what Felipe said he read once."

"Cernunnos had a power like that. Dionysus too," Morven says. "And any new aspects of them would also gain their dying and rising power. Unfortunately, I'm coming up dry on how to turn any of us into a god at the moment."

"Okay," I say, "so let's take dying and killing out of the equation. How else do you pay a life? How else do you sacrifice it?"

"I don't know," he says, a little impatiently. "I'm not exactly the sacrificing type. I've never given up anything in my life, and even when my sister was chosen to wear the crown by our court and I wasn't, I stayed. I didn't even think of leaving home because I couldn't bear to. I couldn't bear to give it up."

Home.

Home.

It hits me like a sear of lighting, like an arrow bolt to the neck.

I step forward.

"What are you doing?" Morven says, stepping with me.

"I have an idea."

"Is it an idea that will actually work? Or is it an idea that's going to end with my sister dead and me being the worst king ever to sit on the antler throne?"

"I have no idea if it will work, but it's all I've got," I say. "Unless you want to wait around for the worst to happen?"

He lets out a heavy, put-upon sigh. "If my sister dies tonight, I will make sure Maynard sings the *worst* songs about you."

"I'd expect nothing less," I say, and then I start walking toward the circle, grateful to hear his nimble, rhythmic footsteps behind me.

The moment we step into the circle, I feel the frisson of power suffusing the space.

Electricity, potential.

Like the air itself is humming, vibrating with a song older than I can possibly imagine.

Morgana's eyes widen when she sees me, and fear—real fear—chases across her face. "No," she whispers. "You're not supposed to be here. You're supposed to be back home. Safe."

Sholto, Idalia, and Ynyr are all watching me, and I notice Morven steps slightly in front of Sholto, blocking the tall advisor from being able to reach me quickly. I'm almost touched by his protective instinct, but then I see the look on Morven's face. It's very plainly an *if you don't save my sister, I will kill you* expression, and that's fair enough, I guess.

I set my eyes on Morgana, and my pulse speeds hot and quick. If I looked beguiling to her when I was bound and spread on the stone slab, then she looks perfect to me now— her hair blowing in the wind, her eyes flashing, the antler torc highlighting her long, graceful neck.

"I'm here for you," I say, my voice pitched so only she can hear. "But I have to know one thing first. Did you always plan for me to be the tithe?"

Her brows lift; her mouth is soft and unhappy. "Yes, Janneth," she answers as quietly as I asked. "From the moment I accepted your bargain. The long year of watching you and wanting you...falling in love with you. I knew what you'd be marked for. What I'd do to you."

It hurts like peeling off a scab, like pulling a splinter free.

It hurts, and yet there's something freeing in it.

She draws in a breath. "Except then you came here, then I truly knew you, and I couldn't do it. I couldn't use you to pay the debt. I..." She puts her hands palm up, almost helplessly. "I love you. So here we are."

I step closer, my heart beating fast but my mind clear, the

air cold and bright in my lungs. There is horror in this place, and there is horror in her, and yet it matches the need in *me*. Though I doubted someone could take me as messy and needy and sprawling as I am, here is the proof.

The queen loves me. Enough to die in my place when she had planned to kill me all along.

"Here we are," I murmur. "Here *I* am. And here I'll stay."

A line appears between her eyebrows, and it's so close to the expression Morven just gave me that I want to laugh. "Janneth," she says. "You must leave. I don't want you to see..." She looks down, and I see at last the dagger belted to her waist. It is sheathed in velvet embroidered with symbols that I don't recognize; the faint sliver of the blade visible above the sheath is dark and dull. Iron.

The only iron I've ever seen in Faerie.

I take Morgana's hands in mine, holding them tight. Mine are cold; hers are warm. She looks at me like she wants to eat me whole and also like she wants to tell me to run.

"I'm paying the tithe with my life," I say, loudly enough that everyone in the stone circle can hear me. "I'm leaving the life of Janneth Carter behind. Forever. My parents are dead, I have no other family, and leaving their graves behind, along with my friends and my work, will come with pain. But the pain is what makes it a sacrifice, and so I pay it gladly."

Morgana's lips are parted in confusion. "What are you saying?"

"I'm staying in Faerie," I tell her. "I'm saying I'm sacrificing my life—except instead of surrendering my body and breath, I'm surrendering my future as a mortal archaeologist, as a friend and as a student." I take a deep breath and meet her gaze once more. "I'm saying that I'm yours, Your Majesty. Utterly and completely. Forever."

The air splits, cracking like glass and then burning like fire. It fills everything and everywhere—the air in my lungs, the space between me and the queen, the tiny space of a gap between her palms and mine. Light spills into the world, lightning forking down from the sky and joining to the trees and the standing stones, making a cage of sizzling heat.

And in that cage, I see visions of realms upon realms upon realms. I see them all suspended in space and time, joined, a tangled skein of kingdoms and dimensions.

And one by one, they vanish from view, tucked away once more.

The sizzling light fades, and the air becomes breathable again, light and easy and sweet. The electric feeling is gone, the ominous clouds are gone, leaving behind stars and a large, pleasant moon.

I look down and see roses have sprung up around my and Morgana's feet. Their dark petals flutter and drift as the breeze tears them away.

We are still holding hands.

"You paid the tithe," the queen says, her face young and open with shock and hope. "You paid the tithe, and no one had to die."

"It was a lucky guess," I say, pulling the queen close by her hands. "I had to try. And now you're stuck with me."

She searches my face. "You know I love you," she says softly. "You know I'd want you to stay here, to live as long as one of us lives, like Felipe has. But you didn't have to—"

"I love you," I say, stopping her right there. "I love you so much it hurts, in the very best way. I love you so much that I still wanted to save you, even when I thought you wanted to kill me. Where you are is my home. For always."

She touches her forehead to mine. "For always," she echoes, her lips nearly grazing my own. "Forever, for the girl who will always want more."

And I give up pretending I care about the people watching us. I wrap my arms around her and kiss her as hard as I can, shivering the moment she gives me her tongue and a taste of fairy fruit.

She tastes amazing, perfect, like a ripe eternity to be taken one bite at a time but swallowed whole. Heaven for insatiable girls; heaven when being hungry is half the fun.

And oblivious to anything and anyone else, I slip my hands into her soft hair and give her all my hunger and all my greed.

Enough to pay every tithe from now until immortal, monstrous, magical, cruel forever.

Thank you so much for reading The Fae Queen's Captive! If you enjoyed the book, please consider leaving a review.

Craving the Sierra Simone version of a fairy wedding, which is obviously incredibly sweet and gentle and normal and stuff? Be sure to sign up for my newsletter to get an exclusive bonus epilogue!

Want to know how the Shadow Market began during this Samhain? Definitely check out The Death God's Sacrifice, which is the story of a gorgon assassin sent to kill a death god... but who becomes his sacrifice instead.

Keep reading for a sneak peek!

"DON'T LOOK AT HER, dipshit. Do you have a death wish?"

I let the barest hint of a smile lift my lips as I strode through the massive stone archway and past the guards who apparently thought I couldn't hear them. The king in this realm refused to embrace the dress and customs of the modern mortal world, so the fortress stood unchanged from mortal antiquity: walls of stone and guards in bronze breastplates and tunics.

I looked out of place in combat boots and black fatigues, but I hadn't had time to wipe the spattered blood from my boots, much less change into something that wouldn't offend the ridiculous king.

I'd like to do far worse than offend him.

"Don't be a pansy. She's got sunglasses on." The bravado in the smaller guard's tone hid the fear I tasted in the air. But now wasn't the moment to savor it.

"I'm not dumb enough to risk it," said the bigger one, looking pointedly at the ground.

A sensible conclusion. Cowardly. But sensible nonetheless.

The stupid, brave one dared a glance in my direction and whistled low. "She don't look dangerous."

Oh, sweetheart...if only I had time to toy with you.

I almost always glamoured my appearance to what it had been when I was human. They knew what I was and yet had seen only a beautiful woman for so long, they forgot what lurked beneath.

The bigger one smacked his counterpart. "That's how she bewitches you!"

I kept walking, eager to finish the job and get my sister out of this hellhole.

They swore I bewitched anyone who looked at me. The weak-minded fucks simply saw an invitation where there was none, and it was somehow my fault when it backfired.

To be fair, I *could* compel them to look into my eyes, but I wasn't running around forcing random people to do it.

When I was younger, I believed them when they said I was bringing the danger upon myself, so I shrouded my face and covered my body, but it was never enough for them to leave us in peace.

I was forced to learn another way. They wouldn't leave me alone when they thought I feared them.

So I made them fear me.

My hard-won reputation had worked for a while, but eventually a reputation grows until warriors want to test themselves against it.

Another set of guards silently opened the doors to the inner chamber, letting me into a cavernous dark room lined with stone columns. I didn't remove my sunglasses; I could rely on other senses to make up for the darkness.

The older man on the throne marked my approach, and I pointedly avoided looking at what was displayed on the wall above his chair. Looking would make me want to puke, and I couldn't afford that kind of distraction right now.

"It's done?" Polydectes, king of this wretched kingdom, asked without glancing up from the parchment in his hand. He played it off as superior disinterest, but I knew better. He was too scared to look at me even if the sunglasses I wore were mirrored enough to make it safe.

Seems we're both avoiding looking at the things that keep us up at night.

I pulled the heavy object from my satchel and held it out. He took it with his eyes still cast down, running his fingers over the shiny stone before he finally processed what he was holding.

His mouth tightened. "Was this *necessary*?"

For that reaction alone? Yes, yes, it was.

"You asked for proof. A trophy. I suppose you'd rather have a head or a heart?"

He pushed the stone off his lap in disgust.

It landed with a cracking sound, but my trophy was intact.

"You truly are a monster."

I ground my teeth at the accusation, fighting the urge to look at the wall above him, to hurl the accusation back.

It wouldn't do any good.

I shrugged, letting him think I was unbothered. They called me a monster but were only too happy to avail themselves of my services.

I was a monster so they didn't have to be.

And I was done with all of it.

"Where's my sister?"

He spread his hands, still looking down at the parchment. "I need you for one more job."

"That wasn't the deal."

"Regardless, you will serve me."

"Have your dog do it." I nodded to the shadows behind the throne. I couldn't see the captain of his guard, but with my heightened senses, I tasted the bitter tang of his treachery, so I knew Perseus was lurking there.

He stepped into the light, daring to look straight at my sunglasses. He was tall and muscular, with a chiseled jaw, a mop of blonde hair, and pale blue eyes.

Scum-sucking liars shouldn't get to be that handsome, but I didn't make the rules.

The king said, "He can't. I need you to kill the Dark Druid."

I looked back and forth between them to see if he was serious. "It can't be done. Not even by me."

His tone grew icy. "Not only will you do it, but you'll do it before he drops the veil between the realms. Or I'll turn Euryale over to my men for target practice."

Shit. *Shit.*

Hunting the most fearsome creatures was my trade, but even I balked at the Dark Druid. He was a half-mad recluse who'd dabbled in dark magic, and now they said he was *wrong*, dangerously unhinged. As long as he got his sacrificial offering to drop the veil between the realms for Samhain every year, he remained within his cave, which everyone seemed to think was a fair trade. An act of aggression against him could be seen as an affront to the faerie Stag Queen since he served her, not to mention the risk of angering the Dark Druid if I couldn't kill him quickly enough.

"Why? He isn't a threat."

"He's a threat to the sacrifices," Perseus said with a grin.

As though he cared about defenseless mortals.

I scoffed. "From what I hear, they aren't complaining." For many years, they'd been sacrificed and never returned. But more recently some sacrifices had reappeared, claiming they'd had a religious experience. Now people competed for the honor, swearing he was a sex god.

People like the Dark Druid didn't change, though. It would only be a matter of time before they started disappearing again, but I wasn't in a position to make that my problem. Why was the king suddenly making it his?

He shifted, clearly hiding something. I could taste his slimy secrecy and reluctance. "I need time to resolve a...situation. I have an unpaid debt to King Darius. If the veil is dropped now, the Shadow Market will open, and his cronies will be able to cross into this realm. When you remove the Dark Druid and bring me his ring of power, I'll have a year to fulfill my debt."

Making an enemy of King Darius was almost as dumb as attempting to kill the Dark Druid, but swapping one enemy for another hardly seemed like a good solution.

"The fae queen isn't going to be bothered you've killed her beast and prevented the Shadow Market?"

He shifted again.

I sighed, feeling older than time. "You won't have killed her beast. I will."

"I'll appease her. She may even be grateful to be rid of him and reward you. With the ring, I can protect you."

He was desperate, and I was expendable if it meant he had a chance of holding off King Darius. If I was expendable, my sister certainly was too. I had no choice but to participate in his ridiculous plan if I ever wanted to see her alive again.

"How do you propose I even get close to him? He doesn't leave his cave, and no one enters."

The smile on Perseus's face sent chills skittering down my spine like rodents. "With the sacrifice."

THE DEATH GOD'S Sacrifice is available now!